TRAPPED

ARMAND ROSAMILIA

SEVERED PRESS
HOBART TASMANIA

TRAPPED

WWW.SEVEREDPRESS.COM

ISBN: 978-1-922551-97-9

AUTHOR'S NOTE

You are about to crack open the sixth book I've written for Severed Press (and you, of course). A quick note about it, and the previous five stories… While you don't need to read the previous five books, it would be helpful, if only to get the back story of the characters in this book.

You see, I've taken a character from each previous book (Dimitri Volkoff from *Ogromny*, Jeremy Shaffer from *The Beast*, Hunter Shaya from *Frozen in Ice*, Jennifer Kelly from *The Sea Was Angry* and Kris Scarlet from *Abandoned*) and tossed them into an airport together. During a massive snowstorm. With a pack of monsters let loose. Do these folks just have bad luck, or what?!

I'll look at this fun story as an alternate reality, where all five of them can coexist and face the dangers.

I hope you enjoy *Trapped* as much as I've enjoyed writing it.

Armand Rosamilia

CHAPTER ONE

It had been touch and go since the weather turned to a sheet of white snow, but Captain Fielding chalked it up to flying in and out of Colorado. He'd flown in worse than this, he reminded himself.

Luckily this wasn't a commercial flight, so he had a handful of military personnel in back with the cargo and Donnie, his copilot, up front with him. Giving him a look.

"What?" Fielding asked. "Don't get soft on me now, kid. We got a plane to land in this blinding whiteout."

"The tower isn't going to let us land in this," Donnie said.

"And they don't have a choice. We're carrying important cargo for the government, whatever it is." Captain Fielding smiled. They were getting a ridiculous amount of money to fly this crate, which meant it was top secret and they didn't want a military pilot in the event something went wrong.

Like trying to land in a blizzard and crashing.

"Flight Eleven Twenty-One, you are not cleared to land," the message came. "I repeat…"

Captain Fielding sighed. "Give them the ID and protocol numbers as instructed. They'll clear a runway."

They have to. We're running low on fuel, he thought. They'd been given strict instructions to land no matter what. The cargo, whatever it was, needed to keep moving. Landing at DIA (Denver International Airport) was only the first step from what Fielding gathered.

He'd been chosen because he'd always been discreet, he was an excellent pilot, and he had a perfect record. He also wasn't stupid, and knew if anything went wrong, it would be his reputation and butt on the line.

Donnie called it in and after a minute of radio silence, while Captain Fielding kept his course and prayed they'd let him land, the air traffic controller got back on the radio. He sounded annoyed but gave them the runway they'd be landing at and said he'd walk them through it. Personally.

"This is going to be fun," Donnie said. He glanced over his shoulder. "I wonder how our packages and guards are doing."

Captain Fielding shrugged. "Not our concern. We're flying this plane because we don't ask questions."

"I know, but I still wonder. Don't you? What's so darn important back there?" Donnie asked, putting his hands up. "I know. I get it. Let's get onto the ground and grab a drink."

Captain Fielding smiled. It would be nice to relax. He hadn't flown in a couple of weeks. His time had been spent in briefings about this flight, but he'd been paid for missed work as well as a nice advance for the next month. He had a paid vacation he wasn't expecting, and all he had to do was fly a bunch of crates to Denver. Easy enough.

Except the snow was getting thicker, visibility a few feet in front of him now. This wasn't going to be so easy.

It only takes seconds, Fielding thought. He was watching his speed and altitude. These days, the plane flies itself with all the technology. Not like the now-ancient planes he'd flown in Desert Shield. He could autopilot this plane to the ground but he preferred to do it himself. Hands on.

That might've been the mistake, because when he touched down onto the runway, the ice and snow piling up too fast to clear took control.

The plane slid to the right, beginning to fishtail.

Captain Fielding took a deep breath and righted it, slowing the plane down and knowing he'd stop it in plenty of time and without incident.

He didn't know he'd overcorrected. Everything on the ground was white, the runway lights buried. The overhead lights dim with the falling snow.

The right wing clipped a snowplow or maybe a crane on top of a snowbank, raising it into the air.

One second the plane was fine and the next it was shaking and spinning, the right side slamming into a snowbank and turning.

Fielding and Donnie were both whipped around, their seatbelts keeping them in place but banging their bodies with such force they were both knocked out.

When Captain Fielding came to, his head was pounding. He felt his forehead and his hand came away bloody. He called out for Donnie but got no answer. The cockpit was dark, the snow already piling up on the windows.

He unhooked his seat belt and stumbled out of the cockpit.

“Hello?” Fielding couldn’t see in the darkness, although it looked like the doors were open. He felt the cold and saw a few snowflakes swirling inside. The door was on an angle and he knew he’d have to reach and pull himself up if he wanted to get out of the plane.

Why don’t I hear sirens? Rescue should be coming, he thought.

He found a flashlight in the supply cabinet and wished he hadn’t.

When he scanned the plane, he saw carnage: blood spattered on the walls. Body parts. Donnie’s upper torso, his legs missing. His eyes wide and unseeing.

The crates had been cracked apart, wood splinters on the floor.

Captain Fielding glanced at the opening again. The snow was already piling up.

He thought he heard sirens in the distance, but it could've been the howling wind.

What had happened to Donnie and the soldiers? The crates?

"Hello?" He knew it was a stupid thing to say, but he didn't know what else to do. As captain, he wasn't going to leave anyone behind. His mind screamed to climb up and out, but he refused until he knew the entire situation.

Something clanged toward the back of the plane.

Fielding moved cautiously, scanning with the flashlight.

The noise came again.

Get out. Get out. Get out filled his thoughts.

He was following a blood trail, which led him directly to…

What in Hell was it?

Captain Fielding didn't have time for his brain to comprehend what the small creature, feasting on the leg of a soldier, was, before it lunged at him.

It wasn't alone, either.

Fielding's screams were cut off as he was ripped apart.

CHAPTER TWO

The spoiled brat seated next to Hunter Shaya was driving him crazy. He kept kicking the bar under the seat, shaking all of them. With every seat taken due to the snowstorm that had swung around and hit the Denver Airport, Hunter had three choices: take it in silence, take a walk and find another seat, or open his mouth and say something.

He chose the last option, leaning closer to the kid. "Stop."

The kid stuck out his tongue and kicked the seat harder. His parents, on the other side, had their earbuds in and were on their phones, ignoring Junior.

Hunter smiled. "Ever seen a Guatemalan beaded lizard?" He took out his phone and scrolled through his pictures. "Cool, right?" He showed the boy the picture. The boy shrugged. "Not only is it the rarest lizard in the world, and not only did I find one and film it for my TV show, but it will also rip your face apart. It will eat your giant stupid ears and wipe that dumb look off your face. Definitely fix your lazy eye, too, you little runt brat. That thing between your legs? It will yank it off so hard you'll pass out. You'll wake up and your fingers and toes will be bitten off one at a time while the lizard pees in your mouth."

The boy shrieked. His parents didn't say a word until he started crawling on them, tears running down his face.

"My work here is done," Hunter said, winking at the couple across the aisle who'd watched it unfold and were both covering their mouths and laughing. "Time for a drink or three."

The bar was crowded. Hunter pushed his way through with a lot of smiles and elbows. He eyed everyone seated and willed at least one of them to leave so he could sit down. He knew with the snowstorm raging outside his flight was likely to be delayed or canceled.

Hunter's small crew was late. He'd flown in from Los Angeles, where he'd had a meeting with execs at some of the top channels like Travel Channel, Destination America, Science Channel and even Food Network to pitch his cable show to a bigger audience. After what he'd encountered at the South Pole a year ago, he knew he needed to strike while the iron was hot.

Not that anyone believed he'd seen and fought an alien creature who absorbed humans. The government had shut him down. Threatened jail time. Confiscated all of his equipment and accounts… until he shut up about it.

Hunter knew people had been paying attention, though, and he wanted to use it as a springboard to work with a company, Discovery Channel and their umbrella shows, who had the resources and could pay better.

"The meetings went well," Hunter said to the guy next to him. "Thanks for asking."

The bartender finally saw him waving and Hunter ordered a draft beer. "Anything local if you got it."

"Even the Food Network pitch about me finding exotic dishes tied to cryptids seemed to work." Hunter leaned toward the guy. "I'm hoping to get a call back. Since it looks like I'll be living in this damn airport, maybe they'll get back and I can hop a flight back to L.A."

The man had been trying to ignore Hunter, but he finally swiveled his chair away and walked off. Hunter chuckled and took his seat.

Four beers later, Hunter was glad he'd found a spot. The lines for the bartenders were six deep in spots. He checked his phone again but he barely had a bar. He was hoping his crew would text or call and let him know where they were. They were flying in from New York with the idea of staying in Denver for a few days and doing an episode about Denver International Airport.

Hunter was fascinated by the things he'd missed despite being in and out of this airport so many times: the demon horse, the apocalyptic murals, gargoyle statues, secret tunnels leading from the airport to NORAD, and a dozen other conspiracy theories.

He wanted to research all of them, and he'd landed in Denver six hours early to do that. Except he'd found a quiet corner on the catwalk at one end of the airport, rolled up his jacket and put his head down and slept for most of it.

The guy seated across from him looked familiar. Maybe a TV exec? Someone who'd worked on his show? Someone Hunter had interviewed?

Another beer later it was still nagging him. The man was in his mid-fifties. He looked tired. His eyes never stopped moving as he sipped a beer and stared at the glass.

Hunter knew he'd lose his seat but he needed to find out who the guy was. He walked off, his body not all the way out of the chair before someone had already taken his spot.

"Hey, how's it going?" Hunter gave the man a warm smile, standing next to him now after fighting through the crowd.

The man looked at Hunter. At first he seemed to look right through him, deep in thought. Then his eyes went wide and he frowned. "Can this day get any worse?" the man groaned.

Hunter was confused but played along. Obviously, the guy knew him. "I'm glad to see you, too. Can I buy you a drink?"

The man stood. "You can keep away from me. I'm not interested."

Hunter grinned. He'd done nothing as far as he could tell but had gotten deep under this guy's skin. "Not interested in a free beer?"

The guy poked Hunter in the chest with a finger. "Not from the likes of you, Shaya. How did you find me? Are you following me, you scumbag?"

Hunter put his hand up. "Woah, buddy. I just came over to say hi. I'm sorry you're having a monumentally bad day. I truly am."

"My lawyer will hear about this."

Hunter wondered if there was a restraining order involved. He didn't think so, although he had a few standouts between former wives, girlfriends, crew and guests.

Then it hit Hunter. "You're Jeremy Schaffer. The teenager who says he battled Bigfoot in New Jersey."

"I want to be left alone," Jeremy said. "I'm not interested in your basic cable show."

Hunter tried to look offended and failed. "I just had a meeting with Travel Channel. My show might be going nationwide, Jeremy. You'd make a great first interview, too."

Jeremy Schaffer shook his head and turned, pushing through the crowd.

Hunter wanted to chase after, but knew there was nowhere to go. Jeremy was trapped in Denver just like Hunter was.

That guy hasn't aged well, Hunter thought. He took Jeremy's seat before someone else could. He tried to remember when he'd supposedly seen a giant monster in some park in the middle of godawful New Jersey. *Mid-eighties? Early nineties? It was at least thirty years ago*, Hunter thought. *I believe him, too, especially now that I see how quickly the government shuts down these things.*

Hunter decided, if he ran into Jeremy Shaffer again, he'd tell him he believed his story and tell him what he'd encountered as well. It could be a bonding moment between the two men, and maybe lead to a prized first interview for the new show on Destination America.

Maybe Jeremy knew how to cook, and they could do an episode of a cryptid cooking show...

CHAPTER THREE

Professor Dimitri Volkoff was getting antsy. There was no way he'd be arriving on-time for the seminar in Atlanta. All of the hours spent working the slides and the speech for nothing. He was going to kill his agent when he saw her. She'd talked him into this.

I'm a scientist, not a public speaker. My findings should be published in reputable magazines, not as a YouTube video, Dimitri thought. *With the new discoveries of the Ogromny in the North Pole... I need to be on a flight there instead of across the country.*

From where he was leaning against the wall, he could see the harsh conditions outside. It may as well have been the North Pole.

Another Ogromny had been supposedly found, although no one had confirmed it yet. Ogromny meant huge in Russian, and he'd been at the head of studying the giant kaiju that had walked out of the Pacific Ocean and stepped on half of San Francisco before it melded with another giant rock monster at Mount Diablo.

It was all very exciting, except it had been over a year since anything had happened. Unless the two Ogromny decided to push apart and step on the population, the grant money was going to dry up.

This is what it's come to: kill people or we no longer care about you, Dime thought. That was his nickname, and he preferred it to the rather formal Dimitri. A Russian by birth but American by choice, he knew the seminar was needed in order to keep his work in the spotlight and keep his team working.

He tried calling his agent but the phone couldn't get a signal. *That's the problem with these massive airports. So impersonal and despite what they say about wanting to be friendly, they were impersonal and cold.*

Dime knew he was starting to get too negative for his own good. Wasn't that why Petra Sokolov had walked away from the project and him? Because he had no patience when it was needed. Because finding and following the kaiju had consumed everything about Dime.

Despite the various TV and print interviews he'd done over the past few months about it, even having to do podcasts like one called *Monster Men*, where the two hosts overwhelmed him with cryptid and horror movie questions, he went unrecognized as he strolled through the airport.

If Nicolas Cage or Britney Spears got ten feet it would be a miracle, even if they wore a disguise,

Dime thought. The fact an actual giant rock beast had crossed the ocean from Russia to San Francisco and beyond was incredible. It turned the science world upside down, although you wouldn't know it from watching television and social media. Sea life had apparently attacked swimmers off of Daytona Beach in Florida. People were missing off of Nagasaki. Aliens at the Poles. It seemed like every week a new creature was being discovered. The kaiju, which he'd called Ogromny in his initial papers, was yesterday's news. Especially since it wasn't doing anything, while Bigfoot and his cousins Sasquatch and Yeti were alive and well and killing tourists in remote locations like the Himalayas, Brazil and New Jersey.

The airport had several bars but they all looked packed right now. Every adult had the same idea: wait out the snowstorm lubricated and in a better mood.

Above his head at this end of the terminal he saw what he'd thought was a catwalk, but it was much wider. A lot of people crashed out up there, using the outlets to plug in their phones. Even without reception, he knew most would be playing Facebook games and passing the time. It seemed like a smart thing to do, but Dime needed to eat something and sneak in a bourbon or whiskey. He'd earned it and it would put him in a better mood.

With only time to kill, Dime went in search of something more nutritious than fast food or a hot dog.

* * * * *

She loved a man in uniform. He was making it so obvious she nearly walked away, showing off her great legs and her butt in the killer blue dress she was wearing.

Kris Scarlet wanted to be subtle. Make this a game. She had all the time in the world right now and as long as the bar had vodka, she'd be fine. She was sure the pilot was going to offer to buy her a drink. She'd make sure he somehow took care of her tab, too.

He was making his move now. He gave her a smile and took his glass of soda to her side of the bar, stopping a couple of feet away. "Please tell me you'll be on Flight 519 to Atlanta," he said.

Kris grinned despite the lame line. "Sorry, Captain…" She looked at his nametag and then directly into his eyes. "Captain Morgan. Ha. That has to be a joke. Right?"

"It's my real name." He was beaming now and put his drink next to hers. "It comes in handy when you need a good pickup line."

"You should've opened with that one instead of the Flight 519 one. It seemed… lazy." Kris turned her head back to her vodka and smiled. "Have a good flight, Captain Morgan."

She thought he'd called her something not nice but his words were drowned out by another announcement about further delayed flights and a couple of them cancelled.

I'm never getting to Seattle at this rate, Kris thought. The work she had to do in Memphis had taken an extra day. She should've changed her flights. Gotten a direct, but she hated sitting for that long. She was bored in this bar, too. Situated at the far end of the terminal, she didn't have many choices to flirt. She thought she'd been too abrupt with the pilot. He would've taken on her tab and more. Not that money was a problem for her. She had her corporate card to play with, and no one was going to question her spending. Especially because of the gray area work she was doing for The Texan.

That was too long of a story to tell anyone, even if she wanted to waste a couple of hours. *No one would believe it, anyway.* Kris smiled and shook her head.

Monsters from an old coal mine killed a bunch of people, including a man I think I might have been in love with. But still ended up with a lot of money and a job with his primary rival, so all's well that ends well, she thought.

As much as she wanted to go for a walk and get something to eat, she knew she'd lose this great seat at the bar. From this vantage point she could see everyone coming and going into the bar and walking by in a hurry to go nowhere.

She was sure, within the hour, every flight would be grounded and she'd be nice and comfy in this seat, watching everyone losing their damn minds.

Kris Scarlet waved at the bartender and ordered another vodka and lemonade.

CHAPTER FOUR

Take a deep breath. This isn't anything to worry about, Jennifer Cross thought. She was trying to move to the newest gate since her previous two had been changed in the last hour. Her flights were delayed and when it was canceled, she'd switched flights.

Now it was also delayed. She was getting jostled by the sheer mass of people and fought to get out of the stream of humanity.

That's when she realized her second suitcase was missing. She cursed under her breath. Had she left it behind where she'd been sitting? She didn't think so. Maybe it had been knocked from her hand by the crowds.

Josh told me to check my bag so I didn't have to carry both of them, but I didn't listen, she thought. *To save a few bucks and because of my own insecurities. Now I'll never find it in this mess, but I have to try.*

The snow was coming down hard outside. As Jennifer started to retrace her steps, knowing it was useless, she wondered if she was going to be trapped in Denver. Didn't Colorado have a game plan for all the snow they got? Maybe this wasn't a big deal to anyone who lived and worked here.

"I've never seen it this bad," Jennifer overheard two pilots as they passed her.

They're not local, though. Maybe they normally don't fly out of Denver, Jennifer thought, trying desperately to remain calm. Now she knew flying to Arizona had been a huge mistake. It was supposed to bring closure about her ex-husband. Tie up the last details. She was moving on with her life, but she could've done it over the phone.

Josh, her new husband, had told her to go. See the property. What her ex had purchased without her knowing. Two hundred acres of land he was in the process of flipping for ten times what he'd paid for it. Enough money to get her out of debt, save a lot of money for her future, and finally relax. As much as she could, anyway.

When she thought of Josh she smiled. They'd been through a lot. The death of her ex-husband (she refused to even think of his name, let alone say it out loud) in Daytona Beach had been horrific… and freeing, too. She admitted it now. He was so controlling she had no money, no way of getting back home, and had been under his thumb for so long. When she'd stumbled into a bar and found people who wanted to help her, it had changed her world.

Josh had treated her like a woman. Like a person who was bent but not broken. He cared about her, was in love with her. He let her sink into depression and tried to help instead of telling her what she needed to do. Josh understood Jennifer.

Her life was better. She had friends. His family loved her. She'd even begun to heal the relationship missing from her own family for all these years while a prisoner of her ex and his rules.

Jennifer got out of the flow of traffic and leaned against a pillar. She wasn't going to find her bag. What if they thought it was a bomb or something? Could she get in trouble? They made announcements all the time about not leaving suitcases unattended. Did they have a lost and found? She hesitated. Admitting she'd left a bag somewhere might create a problem.

Instead, she kept looking. The problem was… it all looked the same to her. Each seat looked the same, every window looked out into a blinding snowstorm, so she didn't have landmarks to remember. Jennifer didn't even know which terminal she was in now, either. The airport was massive.

Sure she'd retraced every step, she finally gave in and went to the lost and found. It ended up being a kiosk with a bored man staring at his phone. After a minute of standing in front of him ignored, Jennifer cleared her throat. When that didn't work, she tapped the kiosk.

The man jumped, which made her smile. He dropped his phone but didn't try to pick it up. "I am so sorry, ma'am. My parents are freaking out over this storm. They keep texting me. I should've never shown them how to text. Deciphering what they're trying to say takes up too much time."

"I get it," Jennifer said, although she didn't. Even though she'd started making amends with her family, she didn't have the relationship she wanted. Not yet. "I lost a bag. I had to change gates a couple of times, and I think I put it down."

"Did you look for it?"

Jennifer smiled. "Of course. If I'd found it, I wouldn't be bothering you." She realized she sounded condescending and snarky. "I'm sorry. It's been a long couple of days."

The man shrugged. "No problem. We're all a little on edge because of the storm. The newest radar says it won't be stopping for a few hours, either. Until it finally blows out of the area. Maybe another twelve hours of this. Twelve more hours of my parents texting."

Jennifer didn't want to be trapped another twelve hours in the airport, but there wasn't another option. The roads would be closed. There was no one she knew in Denver, anyway.

"Can you describe the bag and maybe some of the contents?"

Jennifer gave him the description: a black backpack with a red ribbon tied around the left strap, a silly gift from Josh to remember him when she was on the road. She groaned. “My laptop and phone charger are in there, too. Plus my, uh, women things. Toiletries.”

He started typing furiously. After a minute he frowned. “I don’t have anything matching that description. If you give me your phone number I’ll text you when we find it. Sometimes it hasn’t been recorded in the system yet, or someone accidentally picked it up.” He looked up and smiled. “The good part: no one can accidentally take it with them to Atlanta or Cleveland, since all flights are grounded for the next few hours. Likely a day or so.”

Jennifer groaned. “A day or so? Seriously? I need to get to Boston.”

“I’m sorry. According to the weather, it’s probably snowing really bad in New England, too.” He shook his head. “What kind of phone do you have?”

Jennifer pulled out her phone. It was only at thirty percent. She wanted to kick herself. She knew she should’ve charged it before she packed the charger in the backpack, but thought she’d have time between flights to do it. Even if she had it with her, it seemed like every charging station in the airport was controlled by a family, all fighting to use the units set up.

He put out his hand. “I’m not supposed to do this, obviously, but my phone is charged. I have a charger hidden in the kiosk you can use. It should only take a few minutes.”

Jennifer smiled, maybe for the first time today. "Thank you so much. Can I get you anything in trade? A soda? Coffee?"

"Coffee would be great. I won't get a break today. I'm surprised we've been able to talk this long without a huge line forming behind you." He smiled.

"How do you take it?"

"Britney Spears," he said. Jennifer frowned. He laughed. "I take my coffee light and sweet. Like Britney Spears. It's an old joke I learned from a passenger once. I guess it stuck."

"I'll be right back." Jennifer didn't trust many people but he seemed harmless. The coffee shop wasn't too far away, and it wasn't like he was going to go through her phone or steal it.

She hoped, anyway. This day was getting worse and worse.

Jennifer saw the line to get coffee was at least a dozen people and sighed. Every line was going to get longer as people settled in and had no other alternative but to use the restaurants, coffee shops and bars in the airport.

After what felt like an hour, she got two large coffees and went to the station near the windows for sugar and creamer.

Outside was a blinding sheet of white, snow tapping against the glass.

She could barely see a few feet. If there was a runway and planes out there she couldn't discern them.

The wind shifted for a second, blowing the snow in opposite directions, like the parting of the Red Sea.

Jennifer saw it. A small dark creature with red eyes, fangs, like a sick dog or coyote, running toward the building.

Only a glimpse. Enough to freak her out, though.

Jennifer dropped the coffees and screamed.

CHAPTER FIVE

Great. Someone is freaking out already, Hunter thought. He tried to get the bartender's attention but the bar was packed. It sounded like a woman screaming over near the coffee place or maybe the magazine store.

"Maybe if I flash some cleavage he'll pay attention," the pretty redhead next to Hunter said with a laugh.

He shrugged. "Worth a shot. Do you want to flash or me?" He acted like he was going to pull his shirt off and she laughed.

"I know you," she said, extending a hand. "Kris Scarlet."

"Hunter Shaya." He shook her hand and was surprised by what a firm grip she had. "You might have seen my television show."

"I don't watch much TV," Kris said. "I have more important things to do with my life. Like napping and reading. Killing occasionally." She chuckled. "I'm kidding, of course."

"Of course." Hunter wondered which part she was kidding about. She seemed tough under the feminine look, like a predator. He was going to enjoy this. He was, after all, a big game hunter. She would make a formidable animal to run down and dominate.

Hunter also knew how cheesy that sounded, even in his head. The guys on the crew would have a nice laugh at that stupidity. "So… how do you know me if you haven't seen my award-winning show?"

"What awards did it win?"

Hunter held up a finger. "Award. It was a cable access award for best cinematography four years ago. Not to brag, but we were in some heavy competition against past winners."

Kris laughed. "I had no idea I was in the company of such royalty. Maybe I accidentally saw your award-winning show while channel surfing."

"I thought you didn't watch TV. Too busy killing," Hunter said.

"You can't kill all the time. Some days you need to prep. Make sure your weapons are ready. Get the intel for where the target is and then… you wait for the right moment." Kris bent over the bar and got the attention of the bartender, who came running. "Two bourbons, two beers and two shots of vodka."

"I hope you're sharing," Hunter said.

"Make that three of each and I'll pay." The man on the other end of Kris held up a hundred dollar bill. "I've been trying to get a drink for twenty minutes."

Hunter frowned. He didn’t want this showoff getting between him and Kris. He was enjoying their conversation, their flirting and her cleavage. He stuck his hand out. “Hunter Shaya.”

The man stared at his hand before sighing. “I know you.”

Kris laughed. “Your award-winning cable access show is killing it in Denver, apparently. Maybe travelers can't find anything else to watch.”

Hunter pulled his hand back but pointed at the man. “I know you, too. They call you Dime.”

Dimitri smiled at Kris. “Doctor Dimitri Volkoff.”

Hunter had tried to get Dime on his show for months, but his people ran interference. He’d gotten close to an interview with his partner, Petra, too, but that was shut down by the government. “This can’t be a coincidence. Jeremy Shaffer is also in the airport.” Hunter looked at the crowd around the bar but didn’t see the man. “I ran into Jeremy before.”

“Who’s that?” Kris asked.

“He purportedly had a run-in with a Bigfoot in New Jersey in the eighties when he was a kid,” Hunter said. “The government covered it up, just like they’re trying to cover up the Ogromny that Dime here found.”

“I think it found San Francisco and us,” Dimitri said. “But I can’t talk about it. Just another earthquake hitting the West Coast. Nothing to see. Move along.”

They shared a laugh.

Kris held up her drink. "Anyone remember Forbidden Island off the coast of Nagasaki?"

Hunter and Dimitri both nodded.

Kris chuckled. "They said it was nothing more than a coal fire, sparked when workers started clearing the island for a future resort. But it wasn't that at all."

Hunter slapped the bar and a few people nearby glanced at him. "I knew it. One of the surviving workers told his story on a podcast, about black creatures crawling from the mineshaft. Then he disappeared."

Kris nodded. "Likely paid off. He's living the dream right now in a mansion in Miami or Tokyo. There's a lot of money spent to shut people up. Trust me, I made a great living doing it so far. I also believe everything the two of you have seen is true, because I've seen it myself."

Hunter was about to respond when he saw Jeremy Shaffer walk into the bar. As soon as their eyes met, Jeremy turned to leave.

"Wait. I want to apologize, Jeremy," Hunter said, grabbing the man by his shoulder and leading him back to the bar, purposely putting him next to Kris. "I want you to meet not only my friends but your friends, too. We've all been in it together."

Jeremy nodded at Kris and Dimitri but didn't say anything.

"Can my cleavage get you a drink?" Kris asked.

Jeremy looked at her cleavage and turned away, embarrassed. "I was at the other bar down the way for an hour and never got near the bar."

"What are you drinking?" Hunter asked. "It's on me."

"I just need a beer." Jeremy seemed to be relaxing. "So… what is he talking about, all of us in this together?"

Hunter pointed at Kris. "Forbidden Island coverup." He pointed at Dimitri. "San Francisco earthquake Ogromny tie-in." Hunter grinned. "I survived an alien at the South Pole and you fought a Bigfoot and you're still alive. I think that sums it up."

"What's the chance all of us are in the same bar, at the same time, during a snowstorm of epic proportions?" Dimitri asked. "The only thing worse would be if they ran out of alcohol."

Kris leaned forward and got the bartender's attention. "Since none of us are flying out of Denver soon, we might as well get drunk and make the most of it."

CHAPTER SIX

"I saw it," Jennifer was telling the two security guards. They'd taken her to an office behind the nice man who'd helped her at the kiosk. He still had her phone. Jennifer felt bad because she didn't even know his name, and he'd been so nice to her.

And she'd dumped his coffee when she'd screamed.

"Maybe it was a dog," one of the security guards, a stocky man with a military haircut, said. His last name was Hamilton, according to his name tag.

"Or a coyote," his partner, Barrett, a short thin older man, said with a shrug. "Probably trying to find somewhere warm. Could also be a prairie dog. We see them a lot."

Jennifer shook her head. "No. It had red glowing eyes. Sharp fangs. Thin and wiry. I only saw it for a second, but… it didn't look normal."

Hamilton sighed. "Sounds like a sick animal. We'll do a sweep and find it. No need to panic, or get anyone else excited. This is bad enough being trapped."

She knew they weren't going to search for it, and why should they? She'd screamed like a lunatic. To these two, it was easier to say it was an animal out in the cold than a monster.

A monster? Jennifer sighed. If it hadn't been for the craziness she'd been involved in down in Florida last year, she wouldn't have even believed it was anything but a dog or coyote caught in the storm. But she'd seen too much.

"I'm coming with you," Jennifer said. She took a deep breath. She needed to face this fear head on, like her therapist told her to do. If she didn't go, she'd wonder whether or not her eyes had deceived her. When the two security guards glanced at one another, she clapped her hands. "Let's go, boys. The sooner we check it out the better."

Hamilton looked like a deer in headlights. He slowly shook his head, and Jennifer could see he was trying to find the right excuse so she couldn't go with them or force them to actually do it.

"I won't take no for an answer," Jennifer said. "If I don't go with you, I might blab to everyone about it in the terminal. Maybe I'll see it again out the window. You haven't heard me really, really scream yet, either. I can get even louder."

Barrett sighed. "Fine. Just be quiet. Okay? Follow us at ten feet. Act like you're not with us. If anyone notices you are with us, it might be a problem."

Jennifer agreed and they were out of the office and walking briskly down an empty hallway. She didn't understand why they were so worried until they went through a side door and emerged into a packed terminal area, people packed in like sardines. With nowhere to go, they'd all decided to pick a spot on the floor and crash.

They had to step over and around families as they slowly moved.

"Clear a path," Hamilton was yelling, but no one was listening. "This is a fire hazard. I need a straight path from one end to the other. Come on, people, let's move."

He nearly tripped over a man spread out on the floor, legs splayed and head on a suitcase, watching a video on his giant tablet. The tablet flew through the air and smacked against the floor. Jennifer heard it crack.

"I told you to move," Hamilton yelled as he kept walking. He shook his head. Now people were starting to get out of the way. The man with the cracked tablet was yelling something about suing the city or the airport or someone, but Jennifer kept following and he was drowned out by all the other noise.

"You did that on purpose, didn't you?" Barrett asked Hamilton.

"Maybe. I hate guys like that." They both laughed and smiled at Jennifer when she joined in. "He'll buy another, more expensive one."

They crossed through the sea of humanity and came to another door which clearly stated Authorized Personnel Only. Barrett smiled at Jennifer. "Stay close to us. Don't wander off. There are areas down here even we don't have access to."

"Are you telling me the rumors about this airport being a secret base are true? Or there's a giant tunnel connecting it to a secret military base?" Jennifer asked, only half-kidding. "Are we going to see aliens?"

"Let's hope not," Barrett said. He opened the door and started down a flight of stairs. And another and another. He stopped at a door and zipped up his jacket.

Jennifer could feel the cold emanating from the other side.

Hamilton had his flashlight out. He shrugged. "Let's make this quick. I'm hungry and the cute chick from the coffee shop is getting off of work soon. Today's the day I ask her out."

Barrett glanced at Jennifer. "Don't say chick, man. That's rude. Sorry. My partner is rude. And an idiot."

Jennifer laughed. "No offense taken."

As soon as Barrett opened the door, Jennifer backed up. The cold was unreal, and she didn't have much more than her thin travel jacket. Snow blew inside, whipping around on the strong wind.

Barrett and Hamilton glanced at one another, a look which only guys who'd worked together for a long time would understand. An unspoken 'why are we doing this?' between them.

Jennifer was wondering if this was worth it, too. "Maybe we wait until the storm calms down? I'd hate for one of you to get lost out there."

It was whiteout conditions. She couldn't see more than a foot outside the door, a sheet of blinding whiteness despite it being nighttime.

Barrett popped his head out with his flashlight. "Lemme see if I can find anything, then we'll head back to the office and… hey… I see something."

Hamilton stepped into the doorway, blocking the wind and snow from Jennifer but also her view.

"What is it?" Jennifer asked, trying to look around them and being nosy.

"It's not a dog or coyote," Barrett said. He tried to get back inside and knocked into Hamilton, who went down. "Close the door. Shut it."

Barrett was scrambling backward on his butt, his flashlight rolling away from him.

Jennifer moved to help him but stopped when she saw the dark shape in the doorway.

It was what she'd seen from the window. Red eyes. Thin dark body. Like a dog but not.

It stared at her.

Jennifer could see several more moving in the background.

Hamilton screamed and kicked out at it, while Barrett was trying to stand. He was still yelling to shut the door.

Before Jennifer could decide whether to turn and flee or try to help the men or try to shut the door, Hamilton screamed.

The creature had grabbed the man's leg with sharp claws, ripping through the pant leg like it was nothing. It pulled the man out the door, where two other creatures helped to drag him off into the storm.

One second he was there and then…

The chilling scream freed Jennifer from her paralysis and she slammed the door and locked it.

"No, no, we have to help him," Barrett said, trying to push her away.

"He's gone. We need to call more security guards," Jennifer said. She was trying to remain calm. "We need to call the police. The military. We need someone with a lot of guns."

Something slammed against the door and Jennifer covered her mouth so she didn't scream.

"It might be Hamilton," Barrett said, but he didn't try to open the door.

Another bang, this time louder, against the door, had them both backing up.

After another bang and the door shuddering, they raced back up the stairs.

CHAPTER SEVEN

"Daddy, lookit the doggy," Jetty said, clutching his stuffed kitten. "I think he wants Fluffy."

"Uh huh," his father said absently, trying to get a signal on his phone. "That's nice."

"Daddy, he looks cold." Jetty stood and waved at the doggy outside. It looked miserable, pacing back and forth. Jetty put his head to the glass and looked down. There was a door to let him in. "Do you think he'll want to eat Fluffy?"

"Uh huh," his father said before groaning in frustration. He looked around. "Where is your mother and sister? This is ridiculous. How long does it take to get a sandwich?"

"I'm going to go downstairs and let the doggy in," Jetty said. He smiled. "Unless you say I can't."

"Uh huh," his father said, his head back down staring at the phone.

Jetty wandered down the terminal, weaving in and out of people. Not as many were walking like when they'd first come to the airport. Most were leaning against the wall playing with their phones and tablets. Jetty knew someday he'd have his own phone to talk to his school friends, and a tablet to watch movies. He wanted to watch *Frozen* again, even though daddy said it was a girl movie and not something a five-year old son of his should watch.

Since daddy was hardly ever home until Jetty was already in bed, he got to watch it as much as he wanted. A lot of times with mommy and Floaty, too.

Floaty was his twin sister. Her real name was Fiona, like the girl in *Shrek*. His real name was Jaxson, although he was having trouble spelling it right so far. Mom had told them they were nicknames Floaty and Jetty because they'd been conceived on a boat during a storm, and when they'd found out it would be twins, they joked calling them flotsam and jetsam.

Jetty didn't know what conceived or flotsam or jetsam meant.

He found his way downstairs and was proud of himself for finding what he figured was the door to outside. He'd let the doggy in and play with him. Maybe mommy and daddy would see how much fun the doggy was and let them keep it. Even though daddy said he hated pets and they were worthless.

Jetty smiled and pushed on the door, but it wouldn't budge. He tried to slam his hand on the bar like he'd seen his parents do, but he wasn't tall or strong enough. He hit it and it moved but the door was still closed.

Frustrated, he banged on the door. Maybe the doggy would hear and jump up and somehow open the door. He'd seen magic dogs who could talk and open things in movies. Maybe this doggy was one of those.

The door opened and Jetty laughed. It had worked…

Only it wasn't a door to the outside. And the doggy hadn't opened it, but a man with one big bushy eyebrow who smelled funny, like daddy sometimes did after going out to the garage for awhile on the weekend.

"What?" The guy looked past Jetty and then both ways.

"Hi, mister. I'm trying to find the door to the outside so I can let the doggy in," Jetty said.

The man shook his head. "Where's your parents, kid?"

Jetty pointed at the ceiling. "My dad said it was okay."

"Then you have a horrible daddy." The man looked around again. "You're not supposed to be down here. Can't you read the sign?" He pointed at the sign on the door.

"Not really that good. I'm only five," Jetty said. "The doggy looks really cold."

"What's going on, man? We got a roach left. Hurry up," someone inside yelled.

"Roaches are gross," Jetty said. "Aunt Janet had a bunch in her kitchen because mommy said she was a slob, and now we don't go over there for dinner."

The man grinned. "Different roach, kid. You need to go find your parents and forget you saw me."

"Why would I do that?" Jetty pointed at the man. "I can see you." His eyes went wide. "Are you a ghost?"

The man laughed but it was cut short by a banging noise behind him.

"Hey, man, I think someone's outside," the other man said. "If it's security, we're in trouble."

"Then hide it. Wave your arms and get rid of the smoke." The man turned to Jetty. "Go back, kid. You're not supposed to be here."

Jetty felt the rush of cold air as another door was opened inside. The man let go of the door in front of him, but the wind held it open for a few seconds.

He heard a scream but couldn't tell which man it was. It sounded awful, like he'd slammed a finger in a door like Jetty had done once. That hurt.

Jetty tried to keep the door open so he could maybe help, or at least see what had happened to make him scream.

The other man also screamed and Jetty heard scraping noises and growling, which sounded scary.

He caught a glimpse of the doggy, but it wasn't a doggy at all. It looked like Scar from *The Lion King*, but with even more teeth and claws.

The door closed and Jetty went to try to open it again, but something big and heavy banged against it and he lost his nerve.

If it was Scar, he might try to hurt Jetty or take Fluffy.

There was more banging and screaming on the other side of the door. Jetty decided he was glad he hadn't gone into the room with the two men and the roaches.

"Come on, Fluffy. Let's go tell daddy."

He went back the way he'd come but must've taken a wrong turn, because he wasn't where he was supposed to be. He didn't see anything he recognized and no daddy.

Lost and Found. He remembered mommy telling him if he ever got lost, to ask an adult where lost and found was. She'd know to find him there.

Jetty started walking again, but when he stopped to ask an adult where lost and found was, they were either ignoring him or pretending to sleep.

After walking what felt like forever, he found a spot against a wall no one else was against and put his head down, crying into the fur of Fluffy.

CHAPTER EIGHT

Jennifer and Barrett were running blindly and crashed into several people when they got into the public area of the terminal, suitcases and curses flying.

They went to the security office, both trying to catch their breath. Both trying to understand what had just happened.

"We need to call the police," Jennifer said. She sat down in a chair but when she saw the look of terror on Barrett's face, she got up.

Barrett pointed at the chair. "Hamilton sat there, every shift, watching the monitors and eating his glazed donuts. Every shift with me. I told him he ate too many sweets and it would be the death of him." The man closed his eyes and covered his face with his hands.

Jennifer wanted to cry, but she needed to keep it together. This man had just lost a partner, but there was a lot more at stake. "How does the phone system work? We need to call for backup."

Barrett seemed to compose himself and nodded. He sat down in his chair and picked up the receiver of the phone. He frowned. "It's dead."

Jennifer sighed. "My phone is with the lost and found kiosk guy."

"Curt? He's a good guy." Barrett shook his head. "I don't have a phone on me. We're not supposed to have it because a lot of guys abused it by texting too much." He glanced at the chair next to him. "Like Hamilton. He had this woman he'd talk to, said she was from Singapore or somewhere exotic, and she wanted to come here. He never actually spoke to her, though. Just texts."

Jennifer knew Barrett was losing focus again. "You stay here. Watch the monitors and make sure there's not a problem. Can you do that?"

Barrett took a deep breath. "It's my job, ma'am."

Jennifer left the office and when she walked into the main area, the wall of sound from so many people crowded together hit her. She wondered how many passengers came and went each day, how many people worked in the airport and who else was in and out. The number had to be staggering.

And now something is attacking us, and we're sitting ducks, she thought.

Jennifer got back to the kiosk and smiled at Curt. "Hey… I need my phone if it's charged. Thanks for doing that."

"No problem." He grinned. "And I found your bag, too. Even though you never got me coffee." He clucked his tongue and then laughed. "Are you alright? The boys didn't rough you up, did they? Hamilton can be a jerk sometimes, but he's a good guy." Curt frowned. "Why were you with those guys, anyway? I had your bag, like ten minutes after you… freaked out. What was up with that, too?"

"I am so sorry. I owe you a coffee," Jennifer said. She was looking around, expecting to hear a scream. Maybe the creature was still outside, unable to get in. She took her items. "How are your parents handling the storm?"

"Calls every fifteen minutes now. We're officially snowed in. This is bad, even for Denver. The roads are blocked and the wind is knocking out power and phone lines." Curt shrugged. "If people start to get nasty with me, I'm going to the security room to hide for awhile."

"That might be a sound plan. See you around, and thanks again." Jennifer didn't want to call 9-1-1 in front of Curt or anyone so she waited until she got back to the security office.

"9-1-1, what's your emergency?"

"Hi, yeah, I'm at the Denver International Airport, and there's a creature outside. He took one of the security guards, and, uh, we need help. Lots of it," Jennifer said.

"He took him? Ma'am, you're not making sense."

"Dragged Hamilton outside and we heard… um, noises…" Jennifer saw how upset Barrett was getting again. "Please send help. Lots of it."

"Ma'am… there's a snowstorm. We're trying to rescue several seniors as well as vehicles stuck on the highways. I'm not sure if you think this is funny…"

Jennifer groaned. "This is real. It's happening. A monster is trying to get inside the airport. I'm not pranking you. It's already killed a man."

Barrett took the phone from her. "Hello? Dispatch? This is Officer Martin Barrett, acting supervisor for the security at the airport. I know what she's saying is crazy, but it's true. We have thousands of people trapped here with something very scary with fangs and claws. It's taken Hamilton already, my partner. Please, please send us some firepower." He paused and listened. "Not as far as I can see on the monitors. I don't see a breach, but we can't take the chance. All I can do is gather the rest of the security team and watch the situation, but we need help."

Jennifer glanced at the screens on the wall. A lot of humanity coming and going.

The upper level catwalk was packed with sleeping groups of families, all huddled in their own small spots. You could barely walk up there if you wanted to.

Lines twenty deep at the food kiosks and especially the bars. People were going to drink and eat too much with the stress of being stuck in the airport.

Thousands and thousands of people. She was only seeing a small portion of it on the screens, too. "Are there other security offices?"

"Of course. Five more. Why?" Barrett asked. He handed her back the phone. "Dispatch said they'd send someone, but they don't really believe us."

"They will when people start calling them if it gets inside," Jennifer said, and hoped it wouldn't come to that. Best case scenario would be it can't find a way inside and wanders off. It would be someone else's problem, but it was better than attacking dozens inside the airport.

"What do we do now? Call the other security officers and let them know we have a situation? I need to call my supervisor, but he's not even here today. He's on vacation in the Bahamas." Barrett shook his head. "He always gets lucky."

Jennifer saw a charger bank of radios. "I need one of those to keep in touch with you."

"I can't let you use one. It's against the rules, and if another security guard hears you, they'll question it," Barrett said.

"Good. Because if I have to use it, that means we're already in trouble." Jennifer picked a radio up. "What channel are we on?"

"That's some fancy equipment. It took me weeks to figure it out," Barrett said. He was staring at the screens on the wall.

Jennifer smiled. "This button is for talking and this is the volume so I can hear the response. What channel?"

"Uh, three… but you might need to use it. Look." Barrett took a step back from the monitors and pointed.

At first, Jennifer didn't see what he was pointing at. A movement in a stairwell caught her attention.

"There isn't one of them," Barrett said. "I see a dozen. They're going up and down the stairwell, waiting for someone unlucky enough to open a door."

They were all different shades of black, gray and brown. Mottled spots. Nasty teeth and claws. Thin and wiry like a sickly dog.

"Can we contain them?" Jennifer asked. "Any way to lock the doors from this side or bar them? Put up a *Do Not Enter* sign?"

"We can try. If they get onto any level, we're royally…" Barrett didn't finish his sentence, because a door opened and a man stepped into the stairwell.

He was taken down by three of the creatures, the man ripped to shreds in seconds by the claws and teeth. They tore chunks of meat from the man.

His body fell halfway in and halfway out, giving the dozen creatures access to the rest of the airport.

Giving them access to nearly unlimited meat.

CHAPTER NINE

"Stop calling me Dime. I hate that," Dimitri said, but he laughed and downed another shot of vodka. He pointed the empty shot glass at Kris. "Only she can call me Dime."

"Totally not fair." Jeremy, equally drunk, tried to stand and failed. "What does she have that I don't? I mean, besides boobs and the hair and the nails and the smile and the sexual steam off of her body and the way she talks with the sex like steam from her every word, and…"

Kris put a finger to Jeremy's lips and grinned. "Stop. You're flattering me way too much. Space it out over the next few hours. And stop saying steam, too. It sounds weird."

Jeremy smiled but then slipped off his stool and fell onto the floor. Everyone around them laughed, except for the bartender. "He's cut off. The rest of you might be, too. Maybe take a walk and get some food in you."

Hunter held up the small bowl of pretzels. "I've been eating."

"Actual food," the bartender said. "Time to give up your seats, folks. If you want to get served again, you'll listen to what I'm saying."

Kris blew the bartender a kiss and stood up, smoothing out her clothing. "Time to take this show on the road, boys. Follow me if you want more trouble."

The three men obeyed, staggering behind Kris.

"Where are we going?" Dime asked.

"To find another bar." Kris stopped and the three men nearly crashed into her. She grinned. "Looks like I'm the only one who can hold their liquor. Good to know in my line of work."

"What do you do for a living?" Hunter asked.

"Whatever has to be done and for however much money needs to be spent," Kris said. "I see ice cream. My treat."

Kris was enjoying this, leading these idiots around like the Pied Piper. It gave her something to do besides worry about being stuck in Denver for the rest of her life. Glancing to the side, she saw the snow had gotten even worse outside. It was a glowing white sheet. Was it day or night? You couldn't tell by looking at the windows.

She was halfway to the ice cream shop when a woman nearly ran through her, knocking Kris back. The woman's suitcase was knocked free but the woman kept running.

Kris cursed at the woman. She shook her head. "Some people are jerks."

"Uh, I think we should run," Hunter said. He seemed less drunk than Jeremy and Dime and glanced at Kris. "We're about to get trampled."

Kris threw herself against the nearest wall as a horde of people came flooding in her direction, all of them wide-eyed and scared.

Dime fought through the crowd to stand next to her while Jeremy and Hunter had taken up a position behind a charging station.

The crowd parted like waves around them, and Hunter shook his head and glanced at Kris. "What do you think it is?"

"Something really bad," Kris said. "We should follow them. I'm guessing where they're coming from isn't safe right now."

Kris tried to keep to the wall as much as possible, not wanting to get swept away with the crowd. She'd watched a running of the bulls a few years ago from the comfort of her hotel room, thinking it ridiculous not only to do it, but how you could possibly get caught in it.

Now she knew. The pressure of so many people all going in the same direction, everyone pressed together, as if one person was moving, was palpable. She was in the flow, and kept having to fight her way back to the wall as she moved.

At the next intersection she got a break, because people were flooding to the left and the right with not many heading straight ahead.

Kris headed across, pushing her way as people still managed to crash into her.

The other side of the terminal was calm, people crashed out, most with earbuds and playing with their phones. They all looked so normal to Kris, with no idea what was coming for them.

Kris had no idea, either, but she knew it wasn't going to be friendly and pleasant. She'd heard snippets of dialogue from those running, and it sounded like an animal had gotten loose in the airport. Maybe a rabid dog. Some idiot had brought their pet on a trip and it was sick and angry. She pictured Cujo, with slobber trailing from his mouth, chasing people down.

"Hey, this way," Dime yelled. "I see the security office. They might be able to help. They might have guns, too, to kill whatever it is."

Hunter laughed. "I love you guys. Most people would think it was something simple, but our minds go to the obvious: a cryptid is loose and about to kill all of us. Love it."

Kris sighed and started to follow Dime.

Most of the crowd had passed them now, spreading out to other parts of the packed airport. She wondered what was going to happen when they came to the end. There'd be nowhere to go, and it would rile everyone else into a panic.

She caught a glimpse of three women yelling as they ran, and one of them went down like she'd been yanked off her feet. Kris watched as she was dragged off to the side and caught a glimpse of something that looked like a skinny dog but wasn't. It was…

"I think you might be right, Hunter. I just saw it and it's not a normal animal," Kris said. She ran past Hunter, who stopped.

"Seriously?" Hunter took out his phone. "I need to shoot a video of this for my show. No one is going to believe this."

Kris grabbed him by the arm. "There will be plenty of time to shoot grainy videos that no one will believe later. Right now, we need to get to safety."

As they got closer to the security office, they saw everyone had cleared away except a small boy. At first she thought he might have been trampled to death, but he sat up as they approached. He'd been crying into his stuffed animal.

"Go on ahead and make sure we can get in," Kris said to the men.

"I'll wait right here with you. Make sure nothing happens," Hunter said, but he was looking back the way they'd come with his phone out and ready to film.

"Hey, buddy, are you lost?" Kris didn't think she had much nurturing or motherly bones in her body, but she knew how to fake it. She put out her hand and smiled. "Where are your parents?"

"I don't know. I got lost. I went downstairs to find the doggy, and then it was scary and…"

Hunter had the kid by the arms and lifted him up. "You saw it? Seriously? What did it look like? Describe it for me."

Kris punched Hunter. "Put him down, you idiot. You're scaring him."

“Good idea. I need footage.” Hunter put the boy down and had his phone ready. “What’s your name, kid?”

“Jetty and this is Fluffy.” The boy kept looking around and Kris was afraid Hunter had scared him and he was going to run away, maybe into the jaws of a monster.

“Cool names, kid,” Hunter said. “Now… describe the beast.”

Kris heard something growl back the way they’d come, just out of sight.

“The security office has better lighting,” Kris said to Hunter. She could see Dime and Jeremy had gone inside already. She took Jett’s hand and walked as fast as his little legs would go to the door. She didn’t care if Hunter was coming or not.

CHAPTER TEN

Jennifer smiled as everyone introduced themselves, and she frowned when she saw the state the little boy was in. He looked frightened and confused, which made sense. *He must've seen it*, she thought. *He might be scarred for life*. "What's your son's name?" Jennifer asked Kris and Hunter, who both looked at each other and laughed.

"He's not my kid. No thanks. Nothing against him, but I'm not a father-figure or a role model. I'm just a minor celebrity about to hit the big time," Hunter said. He walked past Jennifer and stared at the camera bank. He whistled. "How many of these things are there?"

Barrett cleared his throat and pushed Hunter out of the way so he had a better view of what was happening. "As far as we can tell, there are twelve of them. They're grouped in twos or threes right now. They've taken down quite a few people, too. A quick bite on the leg to make you immobile."

“Like a piranha,” Hunter said and smiled. “They will bite the fins off of fish and eat one or two a day. Ready access to their food.”

Dimitri sighed. “What are they? Diseased prairie dogs or coyotes?”

Hunter laughed. “It depends on where they came from originally, but I have a definite answer for you, Dime.”

“Don’t call me that,” Dimitri said.

Hunter seemed to see Jennifer for the first time. “I know you. Right?”

“No,” Jennifer said. She definitely knew this crazy man, who had a cheesy TV show about monsters. He’d sniffed around after what had happened in Florida, but he never talked to her or Josh.

“Anyway, what we have in the airport is a goat sucker.” Hunter put up his hands. “That’s the translation from Spanish, anyway.”

Jeremy shook his head. “If you say we’re looking at a bunch of Chupacabra, I’m going to punch you out.”

Hunter put up his hands and took a step back but Kris could see he was smiling. “Calling it like I see it. You can call them whatever you want, Shaffer. You of all people should have an open mind. You fought and killed a Bigfoot as a teenager, Jeremy. Now you don’t believe in monsters?”

Jennifer sighed. She stepped in between the two men before they did something stupid. “Wait. Everyone relax. Whether or not you believe in monsters and cryptids and nightmare creatures doesn't matter. Because we can see them, and they're hunting an airport filled with people. We need a game plan."

"Weapons. We need guns," Dimitri said.

"I have my weapon and that's it," Barrett said. "I haven't been able to reach the other security guards so far. No one is answering their radio." He pointed at the screens. "This is only a small portion of the airport. I can't see most of it."

"We need to leave," Jeremy said.

Kris snorted. "And go where? Into a blinding snowstorm. I'm in heels. I'll take my chances with the goat eaters."

"Goat sucker," Hunter corrected her. "They're going to bite through our calves. Hamstring us. Get us to the ground and then move on."

"And when they get hungry?" Barrett asked. "They come back for whoever's lying around, bleeding out and waiting to die?"

Hunter shrugged. "Pretty much." He got back in front of the screens and began filming with his phone. "This is incredible."

"Isn't there a weapons locker somewhere in the airport, in case of a riot or something?" Jennifer asked.

Barrett shook his head. "You've been watching too many Bruce Willis movies."

Dimitri laughed. He was swaying on his feet. "I think The Rock is a better actor than Bruce Willis."

Jeremy shook his head. “Watch it. Bruce is from New Jersey. My heritage. You don’t talk crap about such a great actor. Ever.”

“Can all of you sober up? We’re all going to die and get eaten, and you’re fighting over which actor is better,” Jennifer said. She was between the two men and shaking her head. This was getting ridiculous.

“Bruce is better,” Kris said under his breath.

“Definitely The Rock,” Dimitri said.

She gave up on them. Maybe if they stayed where they were and watched the monitors, they’d eventually see the National Guard or the police entering. Other people had to have called this in. Right? It might be all over social media, too. Video of these things attacking people.

And then they’d get reposted and someone would claim they did it with CGI, Jennifer thought. *In five minutes it would be forgotten as something new and shiny caught their eyes.*

The boy had crawled under the desk. Jennifer bent over and smiled. “Hey. I didn’t catch your name. I’m Jennifer Cross. Where are your parents?”

At first she didn’t think he was going to talk, so she turned to Barrett, who was seated in his chair, trying to get Hunter out of his way. “Hey, do you have any candy?”

Barrett frowned. “Maybe. Why? I’m not feeding these drunken idiots.”

Jennifer pointed at the boy. Barrett turned his back on everyone and casually opened the bottom drawer of his desk and slipped out a KitKat and palmed it to her.

She handed it to the boy, who stared at it a moment before taking it. He thanked her in a quiet voice and squeezed his stuffed animal tighter.

"We're going to be fine," Jennifer said. "Maybe you can see your parents on the screens."

Barrett shook his head. He made a slicing motion across his throat.

Jennifer glanced up to see people getting ripped apart on most of the screens now, blood everywhere. She ducked her head back down. "Maybe you can stay where you are and eat your candy bar instead."

"I saw the monster. I think I did. It attacked the guy that smelled funny downstairs. I heard it but then the door closed and I ran but then I got lost and was tired," the boy said. "I'm Jetty and this is Fluffy."

"The guy smelled funny?" Jennifer asked, confused.

Barrett leaned into her ear. "Likely Dirk and Ronnie. Stoners who like to take a few hits when it's slow for them, especially in storms. I've yet to actually catch them in the act but they have that definite smell to them. If it wasn't for the amazing work they both did when it was crunch time, I think they would've both been drug tested and tossed out a long time ago. Management might or might not know what they're doing. As long as they don't make my job hard, they can do whatever they want when they're not needed."

Jennifer found herself staring at the monitors with everyone else quietly.

All eyes watched as a dozen creatures tore into the thinning crowd like a hot knife through butter.

CHAPTER ELEVEN

Curt was in the bathroom stall when he heard the commotion outside.

He groaned. *Can't a guy take a dump in peace? What new, fresh Hell is this? I need a new job*, he thought. His sister-in-law had been hinting about an opening at her company, but he didn't want to work in a warehouse and do grunt work. He was out of shape and he actually liked dealing with the public. A few lost suitcases or a phone every few hours wasn't all that hard to figure out.

Even when he was no use to the person with the missing luggage, it didn't really matter. He'd fill out a few forms. Get some information. By the time it was found, the person would be in Seattle or New York and Curt would move the paperwork along with the item.

Boredom was the worst part of the job. He had this fantasy about stealing people's things so he had something to do most days. Luggage getting stolen or lost was actually quite a rare thing. Maybe once a day. With thousands of flyers in and out on a constant basis, that was a pretty low percentage.

Children getting lost was a tough one but he'd frown and nod to the parent or parents, tell them everything would be fine, and call security. Then they'd take over and he'd go back to fantasies of stealing luggage.

The door to the bathroom opened while Curt was pulling up his pants.

Whoever it was sounded rushed, like they really had to use the bathroom. They were banging open the door to each stall.

Curt always used the furthest one from the door.

"Hey, in use," Curt yelled when the person slammed against the door to his stall.

"You gotta help me. They're coming." It was a woman.

Curt sighed. "Miss, this is the men's room."

He looked down to see she'd gotten into the stall next to his and was crawling under the divider into his.

Curt waved his hands. "Stop. What are you doing? You can't be in here."

Was she crazy or high? Maybe she'd been hanging out with Ronnie and Dirk.

She stood and he saw the fear in her eyes. "They killed my family. They killed them all."

Curt took a step back, banging into the sink. That was the other bonus of using the last stall: it was bigger than the others and had its own sink.

"They're like rabid evil dogs," she said, her body shuddering. "It can't be real. It can't be."

Curt went to the stall door to open it but she got in his way, grabbing him by the shirt. She smelled of sweat. "No. Don't leave me. They're coming for all of us. They were right behind me."

"They? Ma'am, you're not making sense." Curt put on a smile and went into work mode. He casually took her hands off of his shirt and took a step back. "I'm sure there's a reasonable explanation for what you saw. Maybe they're filming a commercial or movie today." He knew as soon as he said it how ridiculous it sounded. If that were the case, he would've heard about it.

He thought he heard a scream in the distance, maybe near the closest bar area. Someone getting a bit too drunk. That would be a pleasant flight if they ever got planes back in the air.

She was grabbing at him again.

Curt was about to take her by the arm, as gently as possible, and lead her out of the men's restroom. She wasn't supposed to be in here and he could get in trouble if security saw her enter and knew he was in here. What if she was insane and said he'd tried to do something to her? This wasn't good.

"Ma'am, let's go find out what is happening. OK? I'm sure it's nothing, but we can get you to safety. Maybe someone to talk to. Friends. Family? We'll figure it out," Curt said, babbling. He needed to keep talking and maybe get her to calm down.

As soon as he put his hand on the stall door the main door to the bathroom burst open, slamming against the doorstop.

He froze because with the door open, he definitely heard screaming.

The woman tugged at Curt to move back, her eyes wide.

Something was in the bathroom and it scraped against the tiles. Hadn't she mentioned dogs? Some idiot had let their pets loose in the airport. So many tried to act like their dog was a security animal, when they weren't trained and sometimes got antsy around so many people.

The woman stood on the toilet, leaning against the wall.

Curt heard whatever it was moving slowly and thought he heard it sniffing the air.

He looked around but the toilet wasn't big enough for both of them to stand on. He gingerly put his butt on the sink and tried to spread out without falling, but it was too awkward.

The creature was getting closer, walking next to the stalls.

Closer and closer.

The woman had her hands over her mouth, eyes closed, and she was whimpering. Curt wanted to tell her to keep it down, but he was too busy trying to get back onto the sink.

Click click click across the tiles.

Curt got his butt back onto the sink and balanced himself by pushing his right foot and right arm against the wall and leaning the other way, his left hand pressed against the cold wall behind his head.

He wanted to close his eyes but looked instead.

That was a mistake.

He saw four brown legs, with patches of coarse hair on them. The animal stopped at the door and sniffed.

Maybe the door will hold. It's locked. It might be too stupid to lean down and come under, Curt thought.

It leaned down and came under the door. Curt closed his eyes, because what he was seeing could not be real.

The woman must've opened her eyes because she started to scream.

Curt opened his eyes when he heard her screams go from fear to pain. The creature had either dragged her off of the toilet or she'd stepped down. She was on the floor, her left leg torn apart. It had happened in seconds.

The woman was screaming as the creature crawled up her prone body, jaws snapping and claws slicing her clothes like they were paper.

She got in one last scream before the monster put an arm up and slashed at her mouth three times in quick succession. The woman either fainted or was dead, blood spurting from her face.

Curt looked at the locked door. Did he have enough room to hop off the sink and make it out of the bathroom before he was attacked?

As if sensing his intention, the creature turned and faced him. Blood covered its thick arms and legs and most of its head.

It's now or never, Curt thought. *I can make it*.

The creature sprang at Curt, who panicked and slipped on the sink. He felt the sink itself dislodge from the wall and crash down. He was unable to stop from falling, and landed on the floor and splashed in her blood.

Curt swung his feet out, trying to kick at the creature.

It was gone, a trail of bloody prints going under the next stall and out of sight.

He couldn't hear screaming or any noise coming from outside the bathroom now.

Curt bent down and looked under the stall walls, but he didn't see the creature. He also hadn't heard the door to the bathroom open, either. It was still here, somewhere. Waiting.

He decided to wait. See where the creature was. Take a deep breath.

Curt was paralyzed with fear and couldn't move his body.

CHAPTER TWELVE

"We wait for help," Barrett said. He'd tried calling 9-1-1 but he couldn't get through. So much for an emergency line when you had an actual emergency and no one was going to help you.

"Is this office safe?" Jeremy asked.

"Man, you faced Bigfoot and killed it," Hunter said. "Why are you sweating so much?"

Hunter took the punch from Jeremy in the side of the head, turning a second before he would've gotten it right in the nose.

The small room with so many bodies was now chaos, pushing and shoving, most of them not knowing why.

Jennifer yelled for everyone to stop fighting like little kids.

Jeremy was being held back by Dimitri and Kris. "If he mentions Bigfoot one more time I am going to feed him to the Chupacabra."

Hunter, on the ground, laughed. "I knew you'd see them for what they are: Chupacabra. I like you more and more, but you should work on driving your punch with your body. It will be more effective."

Jennifer groaned at Hunter. "Can't you shut up? Quit while you're ahead."

Hunter shrugged. "Character flaw. I'm also sobering up, which is not a good thing."

Barrett pointed at the screens. "I only see half of them, which means they wandered in search of prey. Out of the area I cover." He smiled. "Maybe they'll all go in different directions and leave this terminal. We might just make it."

"Wait… is that camera on the bottom left right outside this door?" Kris asked.

Barrett put his hands on his head and nodded. He was no longer smiling. If they figured out a way to open the door, everyone was dead. There was no way out of the small room, and nothing to defend themselves with. He had a weapon with six shots.

There were seven of them in the room. If it came down to shooting everyone so they weren't torn apart…

What are you even thinking about? Get focused. This isn't a Stephen King movie. This is reality. Real life but with Chupacabra in Colorado, Barrett thought. *Which, in itself, makes absolutely no sense.*

"Everyone… quiet." Jennifer was next to Barrett now, having pushed past him while he was trying to compose his thoughts. "It's at the door."

Collectively, they held their breath. As if the smallest sound would get them killed, which was probably right.

On the screen, Barrett could see the creature put his front feet up on the door, and could hear it. The sound was loud in the stillness.

It was sniffing, shaking its head back and forth. It knew they were inside.

The creature knelt down and began scratching at the bottom of the door.

The light. It sees the light on, Barrett said. He pointed at the light switch but at first no one understood what he was motioning at. He couldn't push through and shut it himself because he'd need to jostle a couple of people.

He tried to mouth *turn off the light*. Kris and Jeremy, closest to the switch, shook their heads in confusion.

Barrett pointed at the overhead lights and waved his hands.

Kris finally understood and hit the switch, shutting the light off. The bank of screens was more than enough light.

Turning back to the screen, Barrett could see the creature was still sniffing under the door, but it had stopped scratching it. Barrett slowly took off his jacket and handed it across the line of people, and Dimitri placed it slowly on the floor in front of the door. Maybe the rest of the light would be blocked as well as their smell.

The creature began digging at the door furiously now.

Well, that didn't work, Barrett thought. *Now it can smell me. Now it wants to rip me limb from limb.* He wondered if it was like giving a search dog a cloth with the person's smell on it. Would this one follow him until it got a taste? Barrett shuddered.

A second creature joined the first, both scratching on the door. They were taking small chunks from it, but hopefully it would take them hours. Maybe they'd give up in search of easier prey. Maybe the police or the military would show before they were all killed in this office.

Both creatures stopped and looked at one another without a sound.

They're communicating, Barrett thought. *They're not just dumb animals. No wonder they've never been caught or even seen except in a few cases.* He wondered how many of those sightings were actually of the Chupacabra, though. He wasn't someone who spent his time looking at videos of supposed cryptids and he didn't believe in Bigfoot or the Loch Ness Monster.

Hunter was smiling so big Barrett thought the man's teeth were going to spill out of his mouth, shooting more footage of the creatures on the screen and narrating in a whisper.

The two creatures both nodded and began clawing at the door again.

Jetty crawled out from under the desk and stood on shaky legs. He was crying silently, hugging his stuffed animal. "I want my mommy."

Jennifer stooped down and nodded. "I promise, we will find her. We just need to be quiet for a while, okay? Can you do that?"

Jetty nodded and sat in the chair, looking up at the screens.

Barrett sighed. "Maybe he shouldn't be looking at the monitors," he whispered in Jennifer's ear.

She swiveled the chair away from the desk but the boy spun it back around.

The creatures stopped again.

They shared a look.

Both turned and ran off together.

"Something drew their attention," Hunter said. "Maybe the big guns showed up and they'll exterminate the little buggers."

Barrett felt like he could breathe again. If they were going to be rescued…

"That's my daddy," Jetty said, pointing at a screen.

Everyone in the room turned to see.

A man was walking quickly across the airport but stopped and looked behind him.

The two Chupacabra that had been scratching at their door were on another screen, heading his way.

"No. Stay away from my daddy," Jetty yelled.

Barrett went to grab and turn the boy away, but Jennifer got to him first, burying Jetty's face into her body.

They could only watch as the man ran into the men's room.

CHAPTER THIRTEEN

His wife looked pissed, but it wasn't his fault. The crowd had swarmed like locusts and swept him down the terminal.

"We need to go find Jetty," his wife said, which really meant he needed to go while she sat her lazy butt behind the flight kiosk with their daughter.

"Go. I'll watch Fiona." He never called her Floaty. Not even in private. Their dumb nicknames had been cute for about six months, but then it got ridiculous. He could see when his wife would call them those stupid names and everyone would cringe.

It had taken her the first three years of their lives before she stopped with the baby talk, and even when she did it in the bedroom it was not exciting for him.

"I'll stay with Floaty," she said in her little annoying baby girl voice, scrunching up her nose and mouth because she thought it looked cute. It only accentuated her wrinkles. The deep unattractive lines on her face. "No sense in you losing both of our children."

"How dare you…" He threw up his hands and gave up. There was no pleasing her. He hoped the children grew up quickly, so he could leave her. Let her feel the pressure of bills and working. As if she'd ever be able to get a real job. When he'd met her, she'd been a part-time waitress at Cracker Barrel. Barely twenty hours a week.

What was I thinking? I could've dated her roommate, he thought. *I bet she's successful and not a pain at all times.*

Knowing he'd lost the argument before it had begun, he wandered off.

At the next intersection he stopped and looked in all directions. Everything was quiet… too quiet. The overhead announcements had stopped, which was a good thing.

The lights flickered but didn't go out.

He'd been a huge fan of videogames before he'd gotten himself trapped in this marriage. These hallways reminded him of the classic *DOOM*, which he'd spent hours and hours playing.

If a demon from the game popped out he wouldn't be surprised at this point. It would make more sense than the rabid dog things he'd seen.

He'd also watched a woman get torn apart a few feet from his family, before he'd pulled them away and found their hiding spot. He knew it wasn't going to stay safe, especially since he'd seen at least another couple of the creatures since.

There was blood streaked on the floors. Body parts like chewed arms and feet without fingers or toes, as if the monsters had tasted a few morsels to make sure it was delicious.

He stopped and threw up all over the floor, wiping his mouth with the back of his hand and feeling like a coward.

I am a coward. I stayed with her for the children, who I barely interact with, he thought. *Biding my time for what? I need to leave her. Get a life. I used to have one. Friends and Friday night drinks. No one has called me in months, because I'm the lame dad with an overbearing wife. Everyone hates her.*

He thought he heard movement behind and turned quickly. There was nothing he could see, but a scraping noise in the distance told him which way not to go.

What if he found the mangled corpse of his son? He didn't think he could take it. Would he simply keep walking until he was rescued or killed? Right now, it wouldn't matter. Not only did he love his children, he knew his wife would drag him through the coals in divorce court. Take every last penny. He'd been negligent. Her son had been murdered, all because he couldn't keep an eye on Jaxson in a busy airport.

He could hear the judge sentencing him as the gavel slammed on his desk.

Sentencing me? This isn't about jail time, it's about divorce, he thought, shaking his head. He needed to get it together and find his son.

He'd started going away from the scraping noises but now he heard what sounded like bottles breaking to his left. He turned slowly and gasped.

What looked like a black coyote was standing on the counter at a bar, walking slowly in pace with him, knocking off half-empty glasses of beer and liquor as it moved.

Taunting him.

He didn't want to take his eyes off of the creature, thinking he'd read somewhere it was when they attacked, but needing to get away.

A glance to his right and then back again.

The creature hopped off the counter and licked its snout with a thick red tongue.

If I can get to the bathroom, maybe I can hold the door closed until help arrives, he thought. He was no longer wondering about his son because his own survival was front and center on his mind right now.

The creature took a step forward and it was the signal to make a run for it.

He turned and headed for the bathroom, not looking back, knowing it was going to be much faster than he was.

Now he wished he'd skipped all of the big lunches at work and the endless cups of coffee, the cookies and donuts that always seemed to materialize on his desk in the afternoon. The stop off at a fast food drive-thru on his way home, since he wasn't a big fan of his wife's cooking. He'd replaced exercise and the treadmill with extra snacks and his feet up on the coffee table when she wasn't looking.

He hit the door to the bathroom full force, trying to spin back and get it shut.

As he stopped and pivoted, his mind at first didn't understand what he was seeing.

There was another creature, perched on the sink, and it turned its head and might have smiled at him.

Too late, he panicked and flung open the door.

The one that had been chasing him lunged at his legs, and he let go of the door and stumbled backward.

Snapping jaws from both creatures backed him toward the last stall.

Maybe I can get inside and hold them off, he thought, knowing they'd easily fit under the door and bite his legs.

Just as he got to the stall and reached to open the door, a man burst out of the stall closest to the door.

Their eyes met.

He thought he was going to be rescued.

He was wrong.

As if to say he was sorry, the man opened the door and ran out.

The two creatures watched the man go with disinterest. They turned back to him and he knew he'd never get the door open in time. Not that it would matter, anyway.

The last thing he did, before he was ripped apart by the animals, was pray his children were both still alive and would stay that way.

CHAPTER FOURTEEN

"That's Curt," Jennifer and Barrett said at the same time. They'd watched Jetty's father go into the bathroom, followed by a creature, and once the door opened again, Curt had come out running.

Jetty was staring at the screen. "Where's my daddy?"

"I'm sure he's fine," Kris and Jennifer said together. They shared a look, knowing they were probably lying to the kid.

Barrett headed toward the door. "I'm going to save him."

Hunter shook his head. "You'll be killed, just like he's about to be."

Jetty started crying, but Hunter didn't seem to notice or care. He was between Barrett and the door. "That's suicide, buddy. If he runs this way we can hook him in. If he runs the other way…"

Jeremy groaned behind them and all eyes turned to the screens.

Curt was running blindly, and kept looking back.

"Stop worrying about what's gaining on you," Dimitri said. "Worry about what's…"

Curt tripped over a severed arm and went down hard on his knees, his head slapping against the hard floor.

He was unconscious.

"Now I'm going," Barrett said.

"I don't think so," Hunter said.

Barrett pulled his weapon but didn't point it at Hunter. The threat of it being out was enough. "I won't ask again for you to move out of my way."

Hunter shrugged and stepped to his left. "In all fairness, you really never asked me to move. You just pumped up your chest and said you were going."

"He's too far," Jennifer said. She was pointing at the screens. "You'll need to travel across half a terminal to reach him. I see at least two of the creatures right in the middle of us and Curt."

Barret sighed. "This is something I need to do. This is my job, whether you believe it or not. To serve and protect. To help. Right now, you're all safe but Curt needs to be saved."

"Then I'm going with you," Hunter said.

Barrett shook his head. "No. I'll go alone. Two of us will draw a lot more attention. I know this airport like the back of my hand. I'm not going to use the public areas to get close to Curt."

Jennifer was staring at the screens again. "There's nothing close to us. If you're going to go, do it now, Barrett."

Barrett shuffled to the door, turned and smiled at Jennifer. "My first name is Martin. I'll be right back."

"Please be careful," Jennifer said. "If you can't get to him, there's no shame in it. You tried."

"Oh, I'll get Curt back here without a problem. He owes me twenty bucks and I'm going to collect it," Martin Barrett said with a smile but it looked forced.

He was out the door and Dimitri locked it behind him.

Jennifer hugged Jetty, who was still crying. "It will be fine. Your dad is going to be alright. He's hiding, which is a good thing."

"There are still people trying to find a safe place," Jeremy said. "A couple there. And I think one or two hiding behind the kiosk on the far left screen up top."

"Why aren't the military busting down the doors right now to rescue people?" Jeremy asked. He answered his own question. "The snow is getting deeper and it looks like it's picking up. This storm needs to pass."

"Where did they come from?" Kris asked.

Hunter, leaning against the door, shook his head. He pointed at the floor.

"What does that mean?" Dimitri asked.

"Open your eyes. The New World Order built this airport. Masonic symbolism and ties to the Nazis. It's all right in front of you. Don't get me started about the tunnels." Hunter shook his head again.

"Wait… tunnels? Where do they lead to?" Jeremy asked.

"The train that runs between the concourses and an old baggage system for starters, but that's not what is the only thing below us. Far from it." Hunter was grinning. He had everyone's attention. "Underground bunkers. Created by the government in the event of the apocalypse. Built by aliens or maybe the Lizard People. The Illuminati had their hands in it, too. It supposedly goes a hundred miles to NORAD in Colorado Springs."

"Then why aren't we heading to the tunnels?" Jennifer asked.

"Then let's go." Hunter pointed at the video feeds. "Anyone see a door marked *This Way to NORAD* up there?"

"You're a jerk," Kris said. "To think I almost slept with you?"

Hunter's face was red. "Really?"

Kris laughed. "No. You never had a chance."

"We wait for Barrett to rescue Curt and then we get a solid game plan," Jennifer said. She was staring at the screens. "I don't see Barrett but he said he'd be using back hallways."

"Barrett has to know the way to the secret tunnels. Right?" Jeremy asked. "He works in the airport."

"He would have mentioned it then," Dimitri said. "If it's even half as ridiculous as Hunter says, the people who work in the airport aren't getting access to it and there isn't going to be a marked entrance, either."

"We could get killed trying to find it," Kris said.

Hunter chuckled. "We could stay here and then we'd definitely get killed. Six of one, half a dozen of the other. Damned if you do and damned if you don't. Do I need another cliche or two to add to what I'm saying?"

"First things first: Barrett and Curt return safely," Jennifer said. She was back to staring at the monitors. "We can't really do anything until they return. Then we question Barrett. Even if he doesn't know exactly where the entrance is, he must have heard the rumors. He has to know more than we do. Right?"

The room was stifling, especially with so many of them sweating their alcohol out in the cramped space. Jennifer was glad the air conditioning was at least working, but the office wasn't made for so many people in it at once.

Jennifer cursed herself as a jinx when the lights and screens flickered twice before going out, plunging them into darkness.

CHAPTER FIFTEEN

Martin Barrett was sweating profusely, and it wasn't just because the heat was on in the airport to combat the cold outside. He was genuinely scared. His hand shook so badly holding his weapon he was afraid he'd accidentally pull the trigger and shoot his foot.

He stopped and wiped his forehead. Took a deep breath. Needed to get his bearings and figure out how close he was to a service exit to get to Curt.

The boy's father is dead, trapped in a bathroom with one of the creatures. A Chupacabra? Insane, Barrett thought.

Authorized only hallways crisscrossed the airport, making it easy to move around. As long as one of the creatures hadn't also figured out the system, too. People trying to hide might have run through a doorway, chased down by the monsters, and now he'd have to contend with them.

At least I have my keys to get into any of the suites if need be, Barrett thought. He touched his left side, where his keys should've been. He stopped and took a deep breath. He'd left them on the desk. No going back now.

He wanted to check in with the group but knew the noise of even just keying the radio was going to be loud, especially if there was something else in the hallway somewhere. Noises had a strange way of echoing here.

In better times, Hamilton would tell bad jokes and then laugh at them so loud back doors would open to see what was happening. Even doors in another hallway, thinking he was nearby.

Now Barrett thought every footstep was like a gunshot, and he had to stop every few feet in case something was approaching from either end. He hoped the sound wouldn't confuse him, and he'd know which way to run if need be.

At the next intersection he stopped and looked in all four directions. Nothing but hallways, a door every now and then to break up the monotony, and the overhead lights.

And then darkness, as the lights flickered once in unison and went out.

Don't panic, Barrett thought. *The emergency lights will come on any second.*

He stood in total darkness, trying to stay calm. He was breathing too heavily and couldn't hear anything else. He tried to remember where he was and which way he was going to go, but now he couldn't remember if he'd moved when the lights went out and in which direction he'd been facing.

The emergency lights would kick in after a couple of seconds. It felt like he'd been standing in this spot for several minutes, though.

A clicking noise sounded in the distance followed by a second.

Talons on the floor?

Barrett had his weapon out, even though he couldn't see anything. In his other hand was his phone, and he could use it as a light.

Except he was afraid to turn it on and have a Chupacabra ten feet from him, jaws dripping with saliva in anticipation of him being a meal. There might be ten of them, all circling.

Barrett turned on his phone, scanning in all directions with the faint light. He was alone but thought he heard another scraping noise. Was it closer? He had no idea.

He found the flashlight app but noticed he only had thirty percent charge on his phone, and it would drain quickly. If he was correct, and still heading the right way, he'd be out of the hallways in a few minutes.

Barrett moved quickly, staying close to the wall, feeling more comfortable not waltzing down the center and presenting an easy target. Not that he had anywhere to hide if a creature appeared. The back doors to the suites weren't set more than six inches into the wall, making it unusable as a hiding spot.

He kept his light and weapon focused on the door at the end of the hallway, which should lead close to where Curt was lying.

If he's still alive, Barrett thought.

A definite scraping noise echoed behind him, but not nearby. He hoped.

When he got to the door, he opened it slowly. He could see part of the public area with the reflective light off of the snow outside. Not enough to make out more than shapes on the ground. If anything was down the terminal, he'd never see it.

He turned off his light. No sense in giving them a target.

Stepping out of the comfort of the door and hallway, Barrett tried to keep a steady hand on his weapon. He scanned back and forth, expecting to be attacked any second.

He'd come out twenty feet from Curt, who was still motionless.

Barrett crossed to Curt and knelt down, keeping his weapon in hand. Another glance around told him he was safe. For right now.

He checked Curt's pulse and knew he was alive. How badly was he hurt? Barrett didn't want to chance moving him.

Curt was bleeding from a cut on his forehead. He was face down and turned to the side, his mouth hanging open.

Making sure the coast was still clear, Barrett bent down near Curt's ear. "Hey, Curt, buddy, can you hear me? It's time to go. We need to get you to safety."

Curt moaned softly but didn't move.

A crash in the kitchen of the burger joint down the way had Barrett holding his breath.

"Seriously, Curt, I need you to wake up," Barrett whispered. He scanned the area but didn't see any movement. He wondered if the Chupacabra could see in the dark and figured it likely. They seemed like nocturnal predators… as if they even existed an hour ago to Barrett.

Curt moaned again and Barrett put his hand over Curt's mouth.

Another crash in the kitchen.

Curt pushed the hand away and moaned. "Where am I?"

"Shh," Barrett said. He pointed with his chin at the direction the crashes had occurred. "Can you walk?"

Curt rolled over and sat up, shaking his head. He rubbed both of his knees and then the blood off the cut on his head.

"Where are we going?" Curt asked in a whisper.

Barrett pointed at the door he'd come through.

We're going to make it. All we need is to move quietly and get back to the security room, Barrett thought.

Curt took a deep breath and tried to stand, but he was obviously in pain and sat back down. He started to shuffle across the floor.

Barrett hooked Curt's arm and tried to help him up. There was no way they'd be able to get back if Curt slid on the floor the entire way.

There was another crash, but they were already a few feet away. Halfway between where they'd started and the door to the hallway.

To a safer area.

That's when Barrett's phone rang. Loudly.

CHAPTER SIXTEEN

"Everyone remain calm," Hunter said in the dark. "Nobody move. Trust me."

He shuffled toward the door, which he remembered as being to his left. He hoped.

"If that's your hand on my butt I'm going to knock you into tomorrow," Kris hissed.

Hunter laughed. "That's not my hand, although kudos to whoever took the shot and grabbed you."

"Sorry," Jetty said. "I got scared and reached out. I didn't know I was touching you there."

Hunter had his hand on the knob of the door. "Good for you, kid. Okay, I'm going to peek out. Maybe you should squeeze toward the desk and monitors, in case a Chupacabra takes a bite out of my face. Hey, you know there are cameras and flashlight apps on the phones?"

Jennifer had her flashlight app on first and she looked embarrassed. "I guess we all panicked when the lights went out."

"Yeah, well, get situated and then turn it back off. Don't drain your batteries. I have to move the clothing in the door crack and the light might be a dinner bell." Hunter glanced at Jeremy. "But do me a favor, Shaffer: start filming when I open the door. If I'm attacked and ripped apart, I want footage of it for my last show."

"There's something wrong with you," Jeremy said.

Hunter shrugged. "Ready?" He was talking to Jeremy and none of the others. This could be his biggest and last piece of footage. It would make his career, even if it would arguably end it as well.

He opened the door and looked around as far as he could see.

Nothing out of the ordinary. The power was out but the glow of the snowfall outside gave him a few feet to see. Not much, though. The Chupacabra could be sitting a few feet away, waiting for him to step out of the office.

He stepped out, testing to see if they were close and waiting to pounce.

Hunter kept his head on a swivel, but nothing moved in either direction.

Now... where do we even go? I'm not sure why I stepped out here into danger, Hunter thought. He turned back and gave Jeremy a thumbs up, glad the guy was filming.

The power was out everywhere. It might not be confined to the airport, either. What if all of Denver had been knocked out? The police and rescue were never going to come here. They'd be busy with residents. They'd assume the backup power for the airport would be working, too.

He walked a few feet in either direction, careful not to make too much noise.

This is stupid, Hunter thought. He turned and went back inside the office, closing and locking the door behind him.

"What did you see?" Dimitri asked.

"Tons of military, free beer and naked women, but I decided to come back and hang out with you," Hunter said. He was sure he heard Dimitri call him a jerk under his breath. "It's dark. Not as dark as in here, but still too dark to go too far. I don't see anyone. More importantly, I don't see the Chupacabra. Maybe they're in another terminal by now. There might only be a few of them, and I'm sure there are people still hiding. The Chupacabra are finding them. They'll be busy. But… what do we do?"

"We can make a run for it," Jeremy said.

"To where? Even if we manage to get outside, there's ten feet of snow piled up and it's still coming down," Kris said. "I'm not dressed for Denver. I was supposed to be far away from here by now."

"I'm staying right here until we're rescued," Jennifer said.

Hunter nodded, even though it was pitch black and no one could see him.

"I say we take our chances, before one or more of those things figures out a way to get through the door," Jeremy said.

"Chupacabra. Not things." Hunter knew he was correcting Jeremy for nothing, but he felt helpless. He was used to being in charge. Everyone around him was there because of his celebrity, whether it was the crew or whoever he was asking about their cryptid tale. He wasn't used to being ignored or second-guessed. "We'll be rescued at some point. I say we see what happens before we expose ourselves."

"I agree with Jeremy," Kris said. "I can't sit here and do nothing. We wait to see if Barrett returns, and then I say we head for the parking garage. There has to be an SUV with snow tires we can hotwire."

Jennifer laughed. "You can hotwire a car?"

"Of course. I've done it plenty of times." It was Kris talking, and she was close to Hunter. He thought about patting her butt and blaming the kid but he was scared of Kris, who was smoking hot but seemed super deadly, too.

"Besides Jeremy and Kris, who else thinks it's not absolutely insane to walk out the door?" Hunter asked.

"I say we wait," Dimitri said. "At least until Barrett returns. Hear what he has to say. Maybe he knows about secret tunnels, or he saw something we can use."

"That's a good start. What if he doesn't return, though?" Hunter asked.

The little boy began to cry again.

Shut the brat up before they hear his whining, Hunter thought. "Uh, maybe we can comfort the poor little guy so he stops crying."

"Barrett said he was going to take the back way to get to Curt. I saw where he went and it's close," Jennifer said. "I bet we could find our way if we had to. If it comes to that."

Hunter groaned. "I thought you were all for staying in this room and not dying?"

"I am… I think it's smart to have options. When I was in Florida during the… well, when the sea life decided to attack us… anyway… options." Jennifer sighed loudly.

Hunter chuckled. "We're all survivors of something unexplainable. Awesome. When we get out of this latest mess, I want to interview everyone for my show. Sounds good?"

In the dark he didn't know who groaned but it was more than one of them.

Without another word, everyone settled back. They were going to wait for Barrett and Curt. If the two men returned or maybe even one of them, they'd take a new vote.

Hunter wasn't sure he'd be leaving this room, though. Not until he saw it was the only option. Jennifer was right about one thing: options were going to keep them safe and moving to safety. Right now, Hunter wasn't sure what the best plan was.

But he knew the other side of that door wasn't the best one right now.

CHAPTER SEVENTEEN

Barrett's mother was calling.

He scrambled to shut the phone off. To mute it. If it wasn't going to make so much noise, he would've thrown it across the airport.

"I think someone heard," Curt whispered. He'd managed to get to his feet but his knees were banged up pretty bad and he was hobbling.

No way Curt was going to make it to the door if one or more of the monsters came running, alerted to fresh meat by the phone.

Thanks, mom. Even though I told you I was working and I could get my own weather report, Barrett thought. "Stay down. Play dead."

"If they see us, it won't be playing," Curt whispered.

Barrett caught a glimpse of movement about a hundred feet away, a shadow moving through shadows. He dropped down to the floor and tried to remain calm and still.

His body was shaking.

Curt was down next to him, also shivering.

A monster was definitely approaching. Barrett could hear the clicking of its nails on the floor as it moved slowly.

Now he could see it, the small head with overly large wicked teeth protruding from its mouth, sniffing the air as it walked.

It was headed their way and in a direct line with them.

Barrett had his weapon back in the holster. He'd put it away when he'd checked on Curt, not wanting to accidentally fire it. Now he needed it.

But he'd dropped down in an awkward position, and the holster was between his arm and leg. He'd need to swing his arm out and reach down, but then he'd need to lift up his shoulder… it would all be too much.

If it gets within ten feet I'm going for it, Barrett thought.

The creature was fifty feet away and started to move toward the left as it sniffed the air, angling slowly away from them. Would it keep going in that direction, turn back in its original path, or even stop?

Curt made no sound next to him.

This has to work. Being still will keep them away. How long had Curt been knocked out and a sitting duck? If we remain quiet and don't move, maybe it will pass us, Barrett thought.

The Chupacabra was thirty feet away when it stopped. It lifted its head and sniffed the air, its head moving slowly back and forth.

Barrett realized they didn't make any noise other than their movements. No growling, no barking. If they communicated, it wasn't verbally. No wonder they'd remained hidden for so long.

The creature turned to its left and went to the bathroom.

Curt's eyes went wide next to Barrett.

It was the bathroom he'd burst out of.

Barrett rolled over slowly and pulled his weapon. The creature had its back to him now.

The Chupacabra went up on its hind legs and pushed at the door to the bathroom, swinging it open a few inches.

Enough space for two more monsters to slip out.

Barrett could see the remains of what had to be the little boy's father, although it was very dark. It might be his imagination filling in the details as to what he'd actually seen before the door closed again.

There were three of them now.

Barrett held his breath. They'd never make it to the door to freedom. Especially with the shape Curt was in. What to do?

The three creatures all had their snouts in the air, sniffing.

We need a distraction, Barrett thought. *Something to get them away from us. Give us a chance to escape.*

One of the creatures began moving in their direction, too close for comfort.

Barrett moved slowly on his side and prayed he could do this from such an awkward position. He threw his cell phone as far as he could to his right and heard it hit the ground before exploding.

All three Chupacabra ran after it.

"We need to go," Barrett said and got to his feet, hooking Curt by the arm and helping him up as they moved in the direction of the door.

Curt was slowing Barrett down but they were still shuffling along.

Then the lights flickered once. Twice.

The power came back, the backup finally responding.

Not everything was back up and running, but the lights were on.

Machines reset and buzzed all around them.

Curt pulled away from Barrett, seeming to get a second wind, much better than he'd initially been, and picked up the pace.

Barrett was right behind him. He glanced to his right and nearly screamed in alarm.

The three Chupacabra might've been fooled by his phone, but they were charging after Barrett and Curt now.

"Hurry, hurry," Barrett yelled.

Curt hit the door first, pushing it open. He held it for Barrett, who was in and slamming against the door.

"It can't be locked," Curt said in a panic. "It swings open and that's it. We're in trouble."

"No, we're fine," Barrett said, although he knew it was a lie. He braced his back against the door. "Get to my security office. You know where it is?"

"I've been there a million times," Curt said. "But I'm not leaving you."

"You have to or we're both dead." Barrett had his weapon drawn and aimed it at the ceiling. "Go. A bunch of people are hiding in my office. They need help more than I do."

Curt shook his head but took a step back when the creatures started to slam against the door, shaking it.

Barrett smiled. "Either you get lost or I'll shoot you. Curt… don't make me look like an idiot. If I die it'll be as a hero, but if you hang out and bore me, we die together, and I can't have that."

Curt moved toward Barrett but the next strike against the door pushed Barrett a couple of inches before he rammed against the door again.

Barrett heard Curt shuffling down the hallway and hoped he had enough of a jump before the Chupacabra managed to open the door.

It was only a matter of time.

CHAPTER EIGHTEEN

The sudden overheard lights were blinding to Kris, who'd been staring at the dark ceiling for no reason other than boredom.

"Did Barrett do that?" Jennifer asked.

Dimitri shook his head. "The backup power finally kicked on. I'm not sure why it took so long, and I'm not sure it will stay on." As if in answer, the lights flickered but didn't blink out.

Jennifer was staring at the blank screens on the wall. "Will the cameras come back on now?"

Kris knelt down at the computer towers underneath the desk. "I should be able to get them up and running."

"What if it means the military has arrived and thrown on the power?" Jeremy asked.

"All I hear is a lot of what if questions," Hunter said. "I'm going to scout around. We might be sitting here like idiots while everyone is being rescued."

"No one should leave," the little boy said. "My mommy and daddy won't know where I am."

Hunter bent down near the kid. "They don't know you're in here right now."

The little boy began crying.

"What did I say?" Hunter asked, shrugging. "Jeremy, let's go take a walk."

"I don't think so," Jeremy said.

Kris laughed. She'd never met a poorer group of males that thought they were real men. She glanced at them and shook her head. Hunter might be a decent guy if he could get out of his own way, and Dimitri was handsome but self-absorbed in his work. Jeremy had a chip on his shoulder and it had been there for a long time. They were all wrapped up in their own little worlds. If she needed to get out of this alive, she'd need to rely on herself. Maybe Jennifer. She seemed put together enough to not panic if they were cornered.

The wires underneath the desk were covered in dust. No one had been under here for months or years. It was a great thing the system never had issues, but it also meant scraping through layers of dirt with your fingernail and hoping you didn't break a brittle wire.

Kris asked someone to help shed some light and Dimitri obliged, scooting next to her and holding out his phone light. He shined it on her body at first and Kris grinned.

"You can check out my girls later, Dime." Kris waved her hands. "I need the light wherever these two are, not these two." She squeezed her chest and chuckled.

"Sorry," Dimitri said, his face turning red.

Kris waited until he'd composed himself and shone the light where she needed it. A simple reboot hadn't done anything, and she worried the power surge had shorted the system, even though it was built to withstand the exact thing.

"According to my phone, the power is out for miles," Jennifer said. "You'd think Denver of all places would be ready for a storm like this."

"It's bigger than anything they could've prepared for," Dimitri said.

"I need light," Kris said, when Dimitri had strayed as he chatted with Jennifer.

Kris popped open the side of a computer tower using her nails to unscrew the bolts. She held it up and frowned. "Nope. This is fried. I could probably rig a couple of them with parts and maybe, and that's a big maybe, get us back online. I'm sure the internet is out. I'm guessing a few of the monitors themselves might be destroyed, too. If the system is not self-contained it would be pointless anyway." She stood and brushed herself off.

"Where'd you learn to do stuff like this?" Jennifer asked.

"I learn to adapt. To improvise. It's part of the business," Kris said.

"What business?" Dimitir asked, standing.

Kris grinned. "Killing is my business… and business is good." She turned to Hunter. "I'm with you if you think taking a walk will work. We can't stay here and wait to die."

"Who's with us?" Hunter asked.

No one else said a word.

"Chickens," Kris mumbled under her breath. She went to the door. "Don't wait up for us, kids."

"Wait… take a radio," Jennifer said. "I think they still work."

Kris took it but didn't plan on using it. She didn't think touching base with this group, sitting on their hands while she did the hard work, was an option. It was a waste of time. Her goal was to find a way out of the airport, a way to contact the authorities or even kill the threat. It wasn't going to be with any of them, though.

Hunter? Kris shrugged. He might not be too much help other than a distraction for the Chupacabra. Cannon fodder. A tasty morsel for the monsters while she escaped.

"I'm not filming you," Jeremy said to Hunter.

Kris opened the door and looked around. She didn't see anything nasty, so she stepped outside. She slipped off her shoes, which were starting to bother her. She'd be more comfortable in her bare feet. Definitely faster in the event she found herself being chased, or trying to run faster than Hunter.

"You look like you're deep in thought," Hunter said quietly next to her, stepping out into the main area and closing the door softly behind him.

"I am. Thinking about rainbows and puppies," Kris said. "I wish I had a weapon."

"Me too," Hunter said, but Kris thought he'd be more comfortable with a bottle of whiskey in his hand rather than a SIG Sauer P365, her weapon of choice when she could procure one. It always depended on the city she was in and her contacts. "Which way and what are we looking for?"

Kris looked both ways again. With the lights now on it made it easier to see, which wasn't a good thing. There was blood on the floor and it looked like drag marks. For a handful of Chupacabra, they'd done a lot of damage and quickly.

"We're looking for the secret tunnel entrance," Kris said. "And we have a fifty-fifty shot of which way it is, so I'll defer to you."

Hunter shrugged and started walking toward the left. "Do you believe in conspiracy theories and secret tunnels under the airport?"

"I believe in hope and finding a way out of here. That's as far as I'm going to go," Kris said. She didn't want to get ahead of herself. She was going to survive no matter the cost. She had important work somewhere else, and the faster she got out of Denver, the better.

CHAPTER NINETEEN

His knees were still hurting him, and his body felt like it had been on the wrong end of an MMA beating. Curt kept moving down the hallway, and the overhead light wasn't as comforting as he thought it would be. It exposed him to the monsters. In the washed white of the floors and ceilings, under fluorescent lighting, there was nowhere to hide.

Curt stuck out like a sore thumb.

He thought he heard clicking noises behind him, but these hallways were notorious for bouncing sounds. He remembered, about a year ago, thinking he was about to turn a corner on a couple engaged in heavy petting, but he never found out where they were making out. There were so many corners and side passages he'd never explored. It was said you could walk for days without ever crossing a public area.

Curt knew of a few spots where he'd hide when he wanted a break from endless questions from endless people, but he was nowhere near them. He'd spent many quiet moments listening to his music with his earbuds in while eating a ham and cheese sandwich. The last meal he'd had in a dark corner was leftover Rocky Mountain oysters covered in a spicy cocktail sauce. Delicious. It had started because some of the workers thought it was disgusting watching Curt munching on bison testicles. Even though it was definitely a Denver delicacy.

Twice a month he'd have them for dinner and then leftovers for lunch the next day. The only other time they'd complain was when he'd make a tuna sub and stink up the breakroom.

Now they're all dead, Curt thought. He hoped he didn't join them anytime soon. He just needed to keep moving despite the pain.

There was a definite noise behind him but Curt refused to turn and look back. Isn't that how he'd hurt his knees, by taking a peek?

No. Keep moving forward. Don't look back. The Devil is on my heels, Curt thought. He hoped Barrett was fine, but knew it was unlikely. Unless the creatures found another way to get in the hall, he was gone. Curt liked Barrett and Hamilton. They'd both been nice to him, stopping each shift to talk about the Rockies game from the previous night or ask if he wanted something to drink. Genuinely nice guys. And now…

Curt came around a corner and stopped short. At the other end of the hallway was a Chupacabra, standing still and facing in the opposite direction. Sniffing the air.

He didn't want to move and risk it hearing or sensing him, but standing in place until it turned and saw him wasn't an option, either.

Curt did an exaggerated reversal of his steps, thinking he was doing a quiet moonwalk. All those cheesy dance moves he'd tried as a kid were coming back to help now.

The creature kept sniffing the air.

As soon as Curt turned back around the corner, he took a deep breath. If another had been sneaking up behind, he wouldn't have been surprised. Luckily, he was alone, but needed a new route. Where was he going? Barrett had said the security room was safe. He hoped he was right.

With nowhere else to go, Curt got his bearings. He wasn't too far, although he'd need to backtrack to get to the security room. Maybe they had a rack of rifles and an endless supply of ammo like in every horror movie he'd ever watched.

The problem: he knew another one was stalking him.

Curt moved as fast as he could with his body hurting, his shins burning and his knees shaking like they'd fall apart into tiny pieces if he took another step. He turned another corner and rushed to an intersection.

Nothing was coming but he could hear the clicking noises and it sounded like it was behind him. Maybe the one he'd seen had caught a whiff of his pungent fear.

Great. I'm going to die because I'm overweight and I sweat too much, Curt thought.

He didn't know which way to go. Another clicking sound echoed, joining the initial one.

Except he had no idea in which direction they were coming from, just a gut feeling they were coming from opposite directions. Which meant he had an even chance of heading in the wrong or right direction. Knowing the way he'd come wasn't safe and hoping the first creature was coming from that direction, he felt better about his odds. One creature and three hallways to choose.

Curt decided not to go straight, thinking it would lead him back to Barrett and whatever had killed him. Hoping that wasn't true, and Barrett had somehow escaped.

Wait… what if Barrett was still alive? Curt left him for dead.

Feeling a wave of shame coming over him, Curt headed in that direction. Knowing it was foolish. Not able to stop his hurting body from doing it.

CHAPTER TWENTY

Kris wished once again she had a weapon. *I should've kept my stilettos instead of leaving them behind*, she thought. She was deadly with them. Once, when she'd been dating Akira Higuchi, Kris had had a few too many rum and Cokes. She'd gotten nasty with a nosy valet while they were leaving a restaurant and having an argument (about her drinking).

She'd turned, pulled off her stiletto and launched it at the valet before he could react. It had caught him in the nose, slicing his face and dropping him to the ground. Akira had shoved her into his vehicle, paid the valet with a wad of cash, and taken her home.

Hunter was a step ahead of her as they moved. She didn't know if he was being a gentleman and trying to take the lead, or if she was moving too slow for him.

Kris looked over her shoulder, wondering if she could still see her shoes. If they were within sight, she'd go back and…

Two Chupacabra were standing at the office doorway, one of them sniffing her shoes.

My feet don't smell, you stupid Chupacabra, Kris thought. She tapped Hunter on the shoulder and put a finger to her lips.

Hunter followed her gaze and nodded. They increased their pace, getting to the intersection and turning left. Hopefully out of sight of the creatures.

They approached the bar they'd been seated at, getting drunk, a couple of hours ago. Had it even been that long? Kris felt like days had passed since they'd been drinking, laughing and having a good time. Acting like they didn't have a care in the world.

Hunter was looking at the bar, too. She wondered if he'd take a detour.

"We can use the bottles as weapons," Hunter whispered to Kris, who was smiling knowingly. "And liquid courage, too."

Kris nodded in agreement. If they were going to die might as well get a buzz back. They couldn't carry too many without making noise, but one or two might be enough. Having something in her hands would make her feel better, too. Maybe she could find a corkscrew or a knife behind the bar.

Hunter was still a step ahead of her, and as soon as he entered the bar area he stopped.

Kris was about to ask what he was doing when she saw what Hunter was looking at: a Chupacabra lying on the bar. In the spot where they'd been. Was it taking a nap?

The Chupacabra lifted its head and opened its eyes, sniffing the air.

It turned and looked right at them.

Kris cursed under her breath.

"You go left, I go right," Hunter said. "It can't kill both of us."

"I disagree." Kris took a step to her left. "Ready when you are."

Hunter counted down from three and they both took off. For a second, the Chupacabra stared at Kris before turning its head to follow Hunter. It stood on the bar and shook like a wet dog before hopping down to the floor.

Kris got to the other side of the bar and reached over, grabbing two bottles of tequila. Not the expensive stuff, either. No sense in wasting it.

"Where is it?" Hunter asked, grabbing two bottles of whiskey and stepping back. He was looking around the corner of the bar. "We need to kill or be killed before it calls some of its friends. We might be able to take out one of them, but they're fast little buggers."

"I hope your plan isn't to talk them to death," Kris said. She shuffled to her right, away from the bar. She put two chairs in front of her, as if they'd be a shield against the Chupacabra getting at her exposed legs.

Her eyes were also on the area outside the bar. If another one or two showed up they were really in trouble. She wondered if trying to slip out of the side door was a better plan right now. The bar was mostly open, with three short walls of glass the only dividers.

Hunter took a step forward, bottles raised overhead. He peeked behind the bar and shook his head. Kris shrugged but she wasn't going to take a look. Better to sit tight and see if the Chupacabra made the first move.

Which it did, appearing on the bar inches from Hunter's face so quickly Kris would've missed it if she'd blinked.

Hunter fell on his butt, saving his face from a deadly claw swipe from the monster.

Kris knew she wasn't going to reach Hunter in time, so she threw the first bottle in the direction of the Chupacabra. It slammed into half a dozen other bottles lined up behind the counter, smashing them.

What a waste of good alcohol, Kris thought as she charged.

The Chupacabra was distracted, taking a step in the direction of the broken bottles, before turning back to see where Hunter was.

Hunter and Kris both struck at the same time, Hunter as he rose to his feet and Kris as she slid across the floor in bare feet. Their bottles didn't break, but Hunter's slammed into the head of the creature and bounced it off of the solid bar. Kris hit it squarely in the back, driving it down.

They each clubbed it three more times. Hunter's bottle broke on the last strike, but the Chupacabra was dead by then.

Both out of breath, they smiled. Kris opened the bottle of tequila but saw the blood and gore covering the side of it where she'd attacked. She put it on the counter and took a clean bottle, opening and drinking from it before passing it to Hunter.

"Now what?" Hunter asked before taking a swig.

"We search for knives. Anything heavy. I'm taking a bottle of rum with me, too," Kris said. "I'm not sure I want to keep doing this sober."

"Good idea." Hunter started rummaging, putting two knives on the bar. There wasn't much else worth taking. Except another bottle of whiskey, of course.

The snow was still coming down outside. Kris knew rescue wasn't going to come anytime soon. They needed to survive. Glancing at the mess on the counter, she wondered how many more Chupacabra were left. It stunk.

"Time to move," Hunter said and handed her a knife. "We need to find survivors. An exit out of the airport. A good hiding place."

Kris led the way, expecting the fight noises to have called more creatures, but for now it was silent.

We might get out of this alive, Kris thought.

No sooner had she thought it then a Chupacabra appeared in the intersection they'd crossed over from.

"Time to fly," Hunter said and smiled.

"You're enjoying this," Kris said, shaking her head. "There's something wrong with you."

"Remind me to tell you all about the monster I encountered in the South Pole, and it wasn't a polar bear," Hunter said.

Kris groaned. "There aren't polar bears in the South Pole."

Hunter shrugged and took off running.

CHAPTER TWENTY-ONE

Hunter felt like the blind leading the blind, Kris on his heels but no real direction to go other than stay ahead of the Chupacabra. Every terminal and main area looked the same. Inviting and functional for when thousands of people moved in and out of the airport each day. The food and drinks were spaced out in a uniform order but made to look random.

Each sign letting you know whether you were coming or going, and where your next flight or baggage claim was.

Except now the power was back on but the electronic boards were either dark or glitching, numbers, letters and strange symbols flashing and blinking.

"Hallway," Kris said behind Hunter. "Maybe we can find a place to hide and catch our breath."

Hunter thought it was a great idea, because he felt like his heart was going to burst from his chest if he went another five minutes. Between the actual running, which he was never a fan of, and the fear of the creatures dragging him down from behind and ripping the back of his head off, he needed a physical and mental break. Even if it was only for a few minutes.

When he spotted the door leading to what he hoped was a hallway which Barrett had used to find Curt, he ran to it. Hunter didn't point, as if the Chupacabra would see the signal and try to cut them off. He hit the door hard and pivoted. As soon as Kris was inside, he slammed his shoulder against the door. It opened in, so the Chupacabra would only need to put their weight behind it to get in. He knew he could hold off at least three of them, but more than that they were in trouble.

"I need something to hold this door closed," Hunter said to Kris.

The first creature hit the door but it didn't budge with Hunter against it.

Kris ran off down the hallway, trying the back doors as she moved. At the end of the hallway, she looked left and then ran right.

Now at least one more Chupacabra was trying to get in, and Hunter felt them scratching at the bottom of the door.

Hurry up, honey, or you're going to get back to a dead man, Hunter thought.

A third was digging at the door now, only a few inches separating Hunter from the hunters.

He wished he had his phone ready to take video if they broke through. He was still panting and knew he'd get a few steps before they overwhelmed him if he lost his position and they broke in.

"Anytime you're ready to help," Hunter yelled.

The Chupacabra were in a frenzy now on the other side of the door.

Hunter shifted, making sure he didn't slip, planting his feet and his back firmly against the door. He was looking down the hallway.

He saw a Chupacabra at the other end, slowly approaching him.

"Uh, hey, Kris, I have a major problem right now," Hunter said. "I might need some help whenever you can give it. Just saying."

The Chupacabra were pushing Hunter back an inch at a time and he feared he'd lose his grip and fall to the ground.

Not to mention the one stalking him right now. He had the knife in his hand but knew as soon as he stopped putting pressure on the door he'd have a bigger problem.

Hunter took out his phone with his free hand. "Might as well let the world see what's about to kill me. Ratings, here I come."

He got the video running and aimed it at the Chupacabra.

"Smile, you sonofa..." Hunter grinned when he saw Kris coming up behind the creature. The noise of its friends banging away behind him masked her steps. The metal chair in her hand as well as Curt also carrying a chair was a relief.

Hunter measured the distance in his mind and prayed for Kris and Curt to hurry up.

The Chupacabra was thirty feet away, and his would-be rescuers were thirty feet behind the creature.

"Feel free to speed it up a bit," Hunter said.

Fifteen feet away.

They're not going to make it in time, Hunter thought. He needed to decide which item was more important: his phone or the knife. On one hand, he'd have the greatest footage ever and irrefutable proof of a Chupacabra, and he'd be the one credited with shooting it.

But survival kicked in and Hunter tried to slip the phone into his pocket and dropped it.

Groaning, he glanced down to see the screen hadn't cracked and it was still filming.

Maybe it will catch me in a battle against the Chupacabra, Hunter thought. *A life and death struggle. I'll need a good narrator for it, too*.

Hunter looked up to see the Chupacabra rising up to strike.

The others were pushing against his back still.

Knife out, Hunter tried not to close his eyes and failed.

The Chupacabra slammed against his body but he didn't feel teeth or nails slicing his body.

At the sound of grunts, Hunter opened his eyes.

Kris and Curt had taken turns beating the creature with their metal chairs. The Chupacabra was spasming on the ground.

Hunter knelt and stabbed it in the head before picking up his phone and continuing to film as it twitched twice more before dying.

He knew he'd be able to edit it to look like he'd killed it.

The door behind him opened a few inches since he wasn't pressed against it and a claw reached in and sliced the back of his shirt. Hunter fell on his butt.

Curt slammed against the door. "Give me the doorstops," he said to Kris.

Kris, standing over Hunter, handed Curt four doorstops. Hunter wondered where she was hiding them but decided not to ask, too busy slinking down to get a better angle to see up her dress.

She pushed him away with her foot and called him an idiot.

"That should hold for a few minutes," Curt said, stepping back from the door and hefting his chair. "We should probably go to the security room. That's what Barrett said to do."

"Where is Barrett?" Hunter asked, getting up. He ignored the banging on the door from the other side.

Curt shook his head. "He didn't make it. Let's not let his death be for naught."

Hunter shook his head because, despite the sentiment, it sounded like a line from a bad action movie. He started down the hall. "Follow me if you want to live."

CHAPTER TWENTY-TWO

The Chupacabra were back, nails scratching at the door to the security office. They were trapped inside.

Jennifer hugged Jetty when he started to cry. "Shh. We're going to be fine, but we need to stay quiet."

"They know we're in here," Jeremy said. "If it wasn't for a woman and a child in here with me, I'd be crying too." He smiled faintly. "There's nothing else to do but wait for help."

Jennifer used her phone to call 9-1-1. When it connected she got excited, but it kept ringing. She finally gave up, the constant scratching annoying her.

Dimitri sat on the edge of the desk with his arms crossed. He was staring at the door and looked deep in thought.

"What are you thinking about?" Jennifer asked him, hoping for a distraction. Jetty had gone quiet, hugging his stuffed animal.

Dimitri shrugged. "The one that got away. Isn't that always what you think about in times like this? The regrets. The mistakes. Wasted time and lost moments."

"She must've been someone special if she's on your mind during this," Jennifer said gently. She was thinking about Josh, likely going crazy with worry right now.

"She was. Still is, I imagine. Petra. A fellow scientist. We flirted for years but then, after the Ogromny stepped on parts of San Francisco, we took it up a notch." Dimitri looked at the floor. "I screwed it up. I had a good thing going. I couldn't take a minute and have a good time. Give her what she needed, which was my attention. I was so busy with work I didn't realize she wanted and needed more from me."

Jennifer put a hand on his shoulder. "Maybe there's still time."

He didn't respond.

The scraping had stopped.

Maybe they've found something else to hunt, Jennifer thought, feeling awful for thinking about someone else being attacked instead of them. Surely they weren't the only ones left, though. The airport had been packed with travelers and workers. In the panic, a lot likely rushed outside into the snowstorm. She hoped they'd found shelter and had escaped.

The Chupacabra were still inside. From what little she remembered watching cheesy shows about monsters and aliens (and what she knew Hunter

Shaya had on his show) the Chupacabra was from Puerto Rico or South America. Definitely not a Colorado native. It preferred warmer climes… yet it was here, in Denver, during a snowstorm.

"Someone needs to take a look," Jeremy whispered.

Jennifer shook her head. "It's way too dangerous. They might have gotten tired, or changed tactics."

"They're dumb animals," Jeremy said. "Nothing more."

"You can't be sure. No one has ever encountered one before." Jennifer sighed. "I say we wait."

"I fought off a freaking Bigfoot when I was a teenager," Jeremy said. "I lived to tell you about it. You know why? Because we're giving these things too much credit. They're fangs and claws looking for the easiest meal. They went looking for it."

Jeremy put a hand on the doorknob.

Dimitri shook his head. "I wouldn't do that. Wait until Kris and Hunter return."

"They're long gone. Maybe the Chupacabra sniffed them out and they're being attacked right now. We should be out there saving them." Jeremy turned the knob and opened the door a crack. He put his face in the opening and tried to look around.

Jennifer hugged Jetty again.

"I don't see them," Jeremy whispered. "I think we're safe." He gave a thumbs up to Jennifer and Dimitri and opened the door wider.

Then all hell broke loose.

Jeremy took a step outside and screamed. He was pushed back into the room by a Chupacabra, slashing at his legs and slicing ribbons of pants, flesh and bones.

Dimitri rushed to the door to shut it, but Jeremy's fallen body was blocking it.

Another Chupacabra jumped over Jeremy, landing next to his head. Without even looking at Jeremy, it slashed its front claws and blood shot from Jeremy's neck, his left eye rolling away from his ruined face.

Dimitri kicked at the creatures, slamming the door against Jeremy, trying to move him.

Jennifer let go of Jetty, who was paralyzed as he gripped his stuffed animal. She picked up a chair and swung it. The creatures dodged away from it, both now inside the room.

Dimitri nodded at Jennifer as he reached down to pull Jeremy's lifeless body out of the doorway.

Jennifer took another swing, keeping the two monsters at bay. "Stay behind me, Jetty. You move when I move. Got it?" If he heard he didn't make a sound, but as she turned, trying to keep the Chupacabra from getting between her and the door, she could see him shuffling to her back.

Dimitri had Jeremy out of the way, but one of the creatures was trying to get at him.

"I'm so sorry, Jeremy," Dimitri said, using the man as a shield as the creature tore Jeremy apart, trying to get at Dimitri. It was fast, much faster than Dimitri. It was making contact every few strikes, small cuts on Dimitri's arms and legs that were bleeding.

Jennifer tried to swat at the Chupacabra but the other one was lunging at her, trying to find its way around the chair.

"I'm going to rush it and get it past the door," Dimitri yelled. "You and Jetty get out of the room and close the door behind you."

"No way," Jennifer said. "We do this together."

"There's no way we can all get out and then close the door behind us. Save Jetty. I'm going to get them on me," Dimitri said.

Jennifer swung her chair, hitting the Chupacabra back but not doing any real damage. They were just too fast. "No. We do this together."

"No, we don't," Dimitri said, and swung what was left of Jeremy as he pushed forward, angling so both creatures were at him.

Jennifer wasn't going to leave Dimitri to die.

Then she saw Jetty break away and run toward the door.

Dimitri screamed as one of the Chupacabra slashed his left ankle and scraped against the bone with such force Dimitri fell to the floor.

His eyes met Jennifer's and she knew he was pleading not for help, but to escape so his death wasn't in vain.

Jennifer ran to the door, where Jetty waited.

"Go, go, run," she said. As she passed him, she grabbed Jetty and pulled him out the door.

A Chupacabra had already moved past Dimitri and took a bite out of Jetty.

Jennifer screamed but then realized it had gotten a grip on Fluffy, his stuffed animal.

“Let it go,” Jennifer said. “I’ll buy you a new one.”

At first she didn’t think Jetty would obey, but he let go of Fluffy. The Chupacabra fell back, stuffing flying from its jaws, and Jennifer slammed it with her chair.

She managed to close the door a second before one of the monsters slammed into it, trying to escape. They’d switched places and trapped two of them, but at a horrible cost.

CHAPTER TWENTY-THREE

A man screamed behind them, but Jennifer kept running, carrying Jetty now. They'd run through the nearest intersection and saw a few people hiding behind the pretzel stand counter, but they ducked back down.

At least there are a few people alive, Jennifer thought. She wondered for how long, though. The Chupacabra might eventually find them.

Jennifer was getting tired carrying Jetty, but so far she wasn't being followed. If she could find another room to hide in she might be good until help arrived. If it ever arrived. She could see the snow hadn't petered out yet. It looked like it was coming down even harder now, too.

She put Jetty down and tried to push open the women's room door but it only moved a few inches. Jennifer pushed against it.

"Go away," a woman inside the bathroom whispered. "We're packed in here like sardines. You're hitting me with the door. I'm sorry."

Jennifer closed the door. At least there were a few more survivors.

"I can't go in the lady's bathroom anymore. Daddy says I'm too big for that," Jetty said.

Jennifer smiled and took his hand. "Then let's go find a men's bathroom."

"Good, because I have to pee."

They kept moving. She looked back a few times but they weren't being pursued.

Movement caught her eye from above on the catwalk, though.

Jennifer saw two of the Chupacabra looking down at her.

"Time to run again," she said and scooped Jetty back into her arms.

She was expecting the creatures to jump down, but they paced with her from the catwalk. Which was a good thing… but she saw the stairs leading up to the catwalk and she was going to run past it within a hundred feet, in which case they'd be back on her level.

They'd never be able to get much further than a few steps once the Chupacabra came down.

Jetty pointed to the left and Jennifer smiled. "Thanks, buddy." There was a door that should lead into a hallway. She hit the door at full speed and slammed into a woman who'd been behind it, everyone spilling to the ground.

Jennifer groaned, the wind knocked out of her.

She could hear the clacking of claws on the floor approaching, and she thrust her feet out and held the door closed while groaning.

"I'm so sorry, I... Jetty, ohmygod, baby," the woman screamed and hugged the boy.

Jennifer rolled over but pushed against the door again, confused.

The woman was squeezing Jetty tightly and now Jennifer saw a little girl who looked just like Jetty peeking from behind her mother.

"We've been looking for you," the woman said. "Daddy went to find you, but then the things flushed us out of our hiding spot and... I'm so glad you're safe." She looked at Jennifer and mouthed *thank you*.

Jennifer felt the first Chupacabra hit the door. "We need to figure out a way to keep this door closed or this will be a short-lived reunion."

The woman let go of her son and ran down the hallway, opening the first door on the left. "There's food trays on carriers. I wanted to push them and lock the wheels but was afraid with no one guarding the door it wouldn't make sense. Can you hold them off for a minute?"

Jennifer nodded and felt the other Chupacabra banging on the door now, too.

The woman rolled two metal tray carriers, each six foot tall, to where Jennifer was on the ground. They didn't look heavy.

"We need something better than those," Jennifer said. "It will slow them down but I doubt we'd even get to that room before they got into the hallway."

She heard running from down the hallway and cursed under her breath. If another one of the creatures had heard all the noise and came to investigate, they were doomed.

Except it was Hunter, Kris and Curt running at them.

"Need some help?" Curt asked.

Hunter pushed against the door so Jennifer could stand.

"Thanks," Jennifer said. "Where's Barrett?"

Hunter shook his head and focused on the door. The creatures were slamming against it over and over.

Kris and Curt were pushing a large cabinet on wheels, the woman carrying what looked like duffle bags. They seemed to be heavy and she was dragging them.

Jennifer and Hunter held the door until the last possible second and Curt and Kris pushed the tray carriers and cabinet against the door, making sure the wheels were locked in place. The woman dumped the bags on top.

"Curt knows the way out," Hunter said. "We were heading there to make sure it was still clear before we came back for you."

Jennifer hoped they were actually going to come back and not leave. She didn't trust Kris and Hunter to not do whatever was good for Kris and Hunter, but Curt seemed like a nice guy.

"Where's Dime and Jeremy?" Hunter asked.

"They didn't make it. We trapped two of the Chupacabra inside the security office." Jennifer sighed. "We should get to the exit before these two manage to open the door."

The creatures were slamming against the door with such force the heavy carriers were shaking. Even though the wheels were locked, they were still sliding on the floor.

"I'll lead the way," Curt said. "It's actually pretty close. A straight shot at the next intersection to the right and then we find Room 138. It's easy to spot if you realize the numbers are out of place. It should be Room 51, but for some reason they changed it." He glanced over his shoulder as he led the way down the hall. "Room 51… Area 51. It's so obvious. Not sure why they changed it, though."

"Too obvious?" Jennifer answered. She was starting to feel safer, especially with so many in their group now. She saw Jetty smiling as he held his mother's hand, his sister on the other side of the woman.

Kris handed Jennifer her knife and adjusted her dress.

Jennifer had the knife in her hand and was about to tuck it into her waistband but thought better of it. They still needed to be ready for danger. If Kris asked for it back, she'd give it to the woman.

"I've never been through the door, but they say it leads down several flights of stairs to the tunnels below. A girl I used to work with, I can't remember her name, something like Felicity or Felicia, anyway, she saw it open once and five military men came out and locked it behind them. Pretty cool." Curt turned the corner and stopped.

The Chupacabra sprung onto Curt, front claws sweeping across his face and spouting blood from his ruined nose and eye sockets.

It happened so fast it stunned everyone.

Jennifer reacted first, plunging the knife into the back of the Chupacabra over and over.

The monster died but never made a sound.

Curt was dead.

Jennifer stifled a scream and was pulled along by Kris, who was crying.

CHAPTER TWENTY-FOUR

The door to Room 138 had a keypad and also a place for a handprint entry. Neither of them were lit, and when the group took turns hitting buttons, nothing happened.

"Maybe the power trip locked us out," Hunter said.

"Or, more likely, none of us are authorized. We need to bust it down." Kris looked around but there were no other doors in this extension of the hallway. They'd passed a couple of signs that said Level Five Personnel Only. She supposed they weren't authorized to be down here. "It's probably reinforced."

"Stand back," Hunter said, and took a running leap from across the hall, striking the door. It shook but didn't crash in. "That usually works in the movies."

Kris put up her hand. "Do you hear that?"

By the looks on everyone's faces, they'd also heard the clicking noise of Chupacabra nails on the floor. Coming closer. Still out of sight, but she knew they'd run out of time trying to get the door open.

There'd be no time to run down the hallway and hope to find an open door, which was highly unlikely.

Now what?

Kris wished she had her stiletto heels because she might be able to wedge them in the cracks and force the door, or… she didn't know. She was starting to panic, which wasn't like her.

Hunter jabbed his knife into the keypad over and over, but all it did was destroy it. He dug around with the knife to scrape out the wiring, but no matter what he tugged on or cut, the door didn't click open.

"I see them," Jetty said, his voice shaky.

Kris sighed. Two Chupacabra were coming slowly down the hall. They were at a distance, but they'd close the gap quickly, especially if they picked up the pace.

Hunter groaned. "I got nothing else. Can we kick it in?"

"Doubtful," Kris said. She punched the wall next to the door in frustration.

It sounded hollow.

Of course. The door might be reinforced and metal, but the wall was still a wall. Sheetrock and plaster. No one would think to add extra layers on either side, Kris thought. She kicked at the wall with her bare feet. "I need some help."

Jennifer and Hunter joined in, kicking at the wall and putting holes into it. They concentrated on making a big enough hole to crawl into.

Kris glanced down the hall and saw the creatures had cut the gap in half.

Even the kids were now ripping at the wall, breaking off chunks.

Jetty crawled inside and opened the door from the other side.

Not that it would give them a barricade, but it was a start, Kris thought.

They charged in and Hunter, last, closed the door, as if the gaping hole in the wall was going to go unnoticed.

"Down, down," Kris yelled.

Hunter nodded at her and held up his knife. "I'll take the rear and maybe slow them down. Get to the tunnel and get us help."

"Look at you, Hunter Shaya… suddenly a hero," Kris said with a smile.

He shook his head. "Somebody has to do it. Now get going. When this is all said and done, you owe me a drink or three."

"Deal." Kris headed down the stairs to catch up with the rest of the group. She'd need to either get the knife back from Jennifer or hope the woman knew how to use it when the Chupacabra came at them.

Hunter was above her but coming down the steps, too.

"They're coming and I think they brought some friends, too," Hunter was yelling.

With only service lights in the stairwell, it was hard to see more than a few feet below. Kris hoped she didn't step on anything sharp and go plunging down, knocking someone down or hurting herself. Now was not the time to slip and break an ankle.

The stairs descended deeper than she thought they should and she lost track of how many times she hit the next landing and turned the corner to go down again. There were no doors, no markings and nothing different about each staircase.

Just another plunge into the ground.

She could hear Hunter a couple of landings above her. At least, she hoped it was Hunter as the rear guard. She took a glance or two as she turned the next corner, making sure she held onto the railing. It was too dark and she was moving too fast to see anything but shadows on her tail.

We're going to make it. There will be a door and we'll be able to open it and get into the tunnel and survive, Kris thought. She hated the fact she was so scared right now. She'd been in dangerous situations in her career.

"There's another locked door," Jennifer yelled from below.

Kris could hear Jennifer and the mom pounding on it. *I don't even know Jetty's mother's name*, Kris thought. As if it had ever mattered to her in the past. Her career was her life, and she rarely made friends. Names didn't matter because relationships were fleeting. She had marks in her life that needed to be dealt with: killed, robbed, silenced or drained of information. Nothing more than that.

"If we have a problem down there, don't tell me," Hunter said from above.

Kris could hear him getting closer and knew he was being chased down.

She was at the bottom and slammed against the door, hoping to jar it loose. Hoping to knock it off the hinges. Hoping for a miracle.

Hunter crowded in with them now on the bottom landing. Nowhere to go but through a locked door.

Kris looked up to see three Chupacabra on the next landing, taking their time coming down. Knowing their prey was trapped. Sensing the feast they were going to have.

"Everyone throw yourselves against the door and the wall. We can get through, all we need is a break and we can dig through it," Kris yelled.

All we need is a miracle, Kris thought, and slammed against the door.

CHAPTER TWENTY-FIVE

Jennifer hit the door but it didn't budge. Next to her, Kris also had no luck. They were taking turns pounding on the door and trying to knock it off its hinges. No use. It wasn't even moving, and Jennifer thought the noise was whipping the Chupacabra into a frenzy.

At least six of them were above them now, pacing back and forth, waiting for an opening.

Hunter was standing guard at the bottom of the steps, but Jennifer knew if they swarmed him, they'd overwhelm him quickly.

"There are more of them now," Hunter said. "I'd lie and say I'd gladly sacrifice myself so the rest of you can escape, but at this point no one is getting through the door and my death will be a lot of crying and whimpering."

Jennifer punched the door in frustration. Unlike at the door upstairs, the walls on either side were metal. No easy kick through drywall to get around a pesky door.

Jetty and his sister were holding one another behind their mother.

Kris looked as exhausted as Jennifer felt.

Someone from above screamed, not in pain, but in annoyance.

"Hello?" Hunter asked.

The Chupacabra, only a few feet from Hunter, stopped and turned their heads up.

"Anybody down there?"

Jennifer sighed in relief. The military was here to rescue them. They'd be saved.

"We're down here," Hunter said.

"No kidding, dude. I was playing. You had me at hello," the voice said. "I'm coming down."

"There are several Chupacabra cornering us," Hunter said. "A couple are heading back up to you."

"Thanks for the warning, but I am locked and loaded, bro."

The man was getting closer. Jennifer could hear him running down the steps, but the Chupacabra had gone up to intercept him.

Hunter came down to join them at the door. He smiled at Jennifer. "I think we're going to be okay."

Kris shook her head. "One dude and he sounds weird."

"I think that's my friend I met who smells like daddy when he goes to the garage," Jetty said.

His mom sighed and put her thumb and forefinger to her lips, miming smoking a joint.

"Great. A pothead looking for munchies is going to save us," Jennifer said. "Oh, and he has a gun. Even better."

A shot rang out and it was deafening. The children screamed and Jennifer covered her ears but it was too late.

The guy, wearing a jumpsuit, appeared on the landing above them. He looked crazed, his eyes wild and his arm bloody.

Before anyone could warn him, a Chupacabra jumped onto his back and bit down into his neck. Another two creatures attacked his legs.

We're dead. We're all dead, Jennifer thought.

The guy fell back against the far wall, waving his hands and screaming.

And now firing wildly.

Jennifer ducked and nearly got shot in the face, hitting the ground.

Three more shots rang out.

The guy fell to his knees and kept pulling the trigger but he was out of ammo, which was good because he was pointing right at the group.

"The door is open," Jetty said simply.

Jennifer turned to see the door was, indeed, ajar. One of the stray shots had blown out the keypad.

"Run," Kris said quietly and pulled the door open wider. "Go, go."

Jennifer watched the Chupacabra, feasting but with an eye on them. One of the creatures took a step forward.

"Time to go," Hunter said and pushed Jennifer through the door.

They were in a large tunnel. Well-lit. An arrow on the wall pointed to the right.

"The door won't close," Hunter said. "We need to run. Now."

Jennifer scooped up Jetty and his mom grabbed his sister. Everyone started to move quickly, following the arrow.

What else could they do?

"I'm sick of being in the rear," Hunter said.

"Then run faster," Kris shouted over her shoulder. She was in the lead.

Jennifer had Jetty and tried to sprint, but she was tired. Her nerves were frayed. She thought she'd burn out too soon and be overwhelmed by the creatures.

She couldn't hear if they were in pursuit over her own heavy breathing and her pounding heartbeat as well as Jetty whimpering in her arms.

"They're getting closer," Jetty said into her ear, hanging over her left shoulder now. "Mister Hunter needs to run faster."

"Run, Hunter," Jennifer shouted, careful not to turn and lose her balance.

The tunnel had a slight curve to the left up ahead, but otherwise it all looked the same.

You can drive an eighteen-wheeler down this tunnel, Jennifer thought, *and still have room for a car next to it.*

Jennifer tried to distract herself from the danger on her heels, noticing there were no doors. No other markings on the walls. The overhead lights kept the tunnel fully lit, with no shadows. Nowhere to hide.

Hunter was next to her now, panting as hard as she was. He gave her a quick look and nodded.

Jennifer tried to speed up and failed. Jetty's mom and sister were a few steps ahead and Kris was opening a gap between all of them. She was going to be out of sight in a few minutes at this pace.

Don't look back, Jennifer kept thinking over and over. If the Chupacabra caught up and knocked her down, she'd need to get between them and Jetty. Keep him safe for as long as possible. Hope he could escape while she was torn apart.

Kris stopped short ahead, nearly out of sight. She fell to the ground as if she'd been shot and yelled out, "Down. Everyone get down. Now. Hurry."

CHAPTER TWENTY-SIX

Jennifer fell to the hard ground a second before a hail of bullets whizzed past. She cradled Jetty and tried to protect him, knowing her flesh and bones wasn't much protection against a bullet.

Hunter screamed behind her and she glanced back to see he was bleeding a few feet away, a bloom of crimson on his shoulder. He grimaced and crawled toward her.

Who was shooting? Where were the Chupacabra? What was going on?

She was curious but not enough to lift her head up and risk death.

Jetty was crying. His sister was crying.

Out of the frying pan and into the fire, Jennifer thought. She had her eyes closed now, buried under her hair and into the neck of Jetty underneath her.

Hunter groaned but that was a good sign. It meant he was still alive. It meant he wasn't dead from a bullet and the Chupacabra hadn't taken a chunk from him yet, either.

She could smell the rotten egg stench of so many weapons being fired at once. How many? Her brain couldn't wrap around the number. She hadn't actually seen a shooter, either. Just Kris falling down and the feel of projectiles headed in her direction.

Whoever it was who'd fired were reckless.

Had they been saved, or were they going to be in even deeper trouble? As if being chased by mythical creatures from the jungles wasn't bad enough.

Her ears were ringing and her heart was thumping. The noise from the gunshots in the stairwell had left her with a headache, and even in such a large space, the noise had been deafening.

She thought she asked Jetty if he was okay, but if she'd spoken, she couldn't hear herself.

The white noise was unbearable, like she'd been to a heavy metal concert and pressed her ears to the speakers.

Kris stood and put her hands in the air.

Jennifer still couldn't see who had fired.

Hunter was standing, cradling his wounded bleeding shoulder and looking pale.

Jetty's mother rose, clutching her daughter, and ran to Jennifer, who released Jetty and stood slowly. The woman was saying something but Jennifer couldn't hear what she was saying. By the look on her face, though, Jennifer knew she was being thanked for shielding her child.

A dozen armed men and women in military uniforms came into view, all marching in a line across the tunnel.

Jennifer turned back to see the Chupacabra, torn apart by the bullets. Pieces of them scattered across the floor, a couple further back. Maybe they'd tried to retreat. She hoped they'd all been killed.

Hunter went down to one knee.

The soldiers had put their weapons over a shoulder and rushed to the group. Not in a threatening manner.

To help, especially Hunter. They laid him down and ripped his shirt off, tying off the blood flow.

Jennifer was led away with the rest of the survivors down the tunnel, maybe a quarter of a mile. As they rounded the bend, she saw another dozen armed soldiers standing at the ready near a military truck.

A woman was talking to Jennifer, who shook her head and pointed at her ears. The woman smiled and led her to the back of the truck, helping her inside.

Jennifer watched as everyone was loaded into the truck and the armed soldiers ran off down the tunnel. She hoped they'd be thorough and find if any more of the creatures were still alive.

An hour later, with her hearing mostly returned and only a dull static noise working on an even bigger headache, Jennifer was given a bottle of water and a bag of potato chips. She sat with the others in a nondescript room, all except for Hunter, who'd been led away on a stretcher. He'd smiled and given them a thumbs up.

Everyone was exhausted, and the kid's mother had her eyes closed but her arms wrapped around her children.

Kris was trying unsuccessfully to straighten her hair with her fingers.

The door opened and an older military man with requisite buzz cut and steely eyes entered, standing at attention. "We'll be debriefing everyone one at a time." He turned to Jennifer. "Ma'am, please come with me."

Too tired to argue and still feeling like she was in shock, Jennifer complied. She followed at a distance and tried to keep up with his fast pace. They were in a building of some sort and hallways crisscrossed every hundred feet, but there were no windows and the doors were closed with keypads. No signs announcing what was beyond the door, and no markings on the floor or walls. Just an endless whiteness of walls, ceilings and floors.

"Where are we?" Jennifer asked, but if he heard he ignored her, leading her for nearly ten minutes until she felt lost. He stopped next to a door to his right, opened it, and motioned her inside.

Jennifer walked into a room similar to the one she'd been in previously. The military man closed the door without stepping inside.

She was alone, although there was a video screen on the far wall and one chair facing it.

"Please sit, Jennifer Cross," a voice said. "Can I get you anything? A Coke? A sandwich?"

"I'm fine." Jennifer sat down and the screen lit up, showing a group of three men and a woman in white lab coats seated at a desk. They introduced themselves and all smiled.

"You've been through quite a traumatic experience," the woman said. "Surreal. Unreal. As time passes, you'll figure out what you actually saw and what you think you saw."

Jennifer sighed. "Can you get to the point? Not to be rude, but I want to go home."

The woman smiled wider and nodded. "Of course. This won't take more than a few minutes. We have a plane waiting to take you home. Everyone will be safe within a few hours."

"Until then…?" Jennifer knew what this was and what they'd ask of her. She didn't care. All she wanted was to be reunited with Josh and live the rest of her life, without strange monsters trying to kill her. She decided to stay at home for as long as possible and not leave the house unless absolutely necessary. Luckily, Josh would know exactly what had happened, since he'd shared in her previous encounter.

"We have some tests to conduct. Nothing too invasive," the woman said. "Then a few forms to sign."

"A stack of forms so I keep my mouth shut. So I'm not on the six o'clock news talking about Chupacabra attacking us," Jennifer said.

The woman chuckled. "You're referring to the pack of wild feral dogs loose in the airport, looking for warmth and shelter. Nothing more."

Jennifer stood. "I get it. You'll get no fight from me. I just want to go home. Give me a pen so I can sign and head out."

"Very well. Go through the door and turn to your right," the woman said.

Jennifer held up her hand. "Can you at least tell me where I am? Is this a secret military base? A FEMA outpost? A bomb shelter for the government?"

The woman stopped smiling and glanced at her companions, who'd remained quiet. "I don't know what you mean. We're not underground. There are no tunnels. No secrets under the Denver International Airport. You're being debriefed in a security room above ground. As you shall read about in the papers you sign, ma'am."

CHAPTER TWENTY-SEVEN

It had never felt such coldness in its short life, and it shivered as it dragged the warm carcass across the runway and into the field. Snow piled up around it, covering the drag marks and its own tracks.

They'd survived for decades in secret, only venturing forth when the humans had entered their territory and begun to chop down their habitat.

When it had finally escaped from the airplane, the others had already scattered. Gotten inside the warm building. Found food.

The darkness was absolute in the falling snow, and it interfered with its natural vision to see in the dark. Everything was distorted.

Dragging the body down into what was a runoff ditch in nicer weather, it decided to feast first and then enter the carcass for warmth.

Wait until the snow melted. Warmer weather. Create a new territory. Find a remote area and live. Thrive. It could feel the children inside, yearning to survive as well.

The others would eventually find the new colony. If not, they'd create a new one. Travel to warmer climes at some point, if they survived.

It knew they'd hunt it. Already lights and vehicles surrounded the building. When they'd been cornered and captured originally, it seemed like they'd be killed. Instead, they'd been put into crates and into the sky.

The snow was falling even worse now, coating its fur and seeping into its warm body. An annoyance and nothing more. It needed to survive and the cold wasn't going to kill it.

Not with the carcass in its teeth.

It ripped apart the white shirt of the man and burrowed inside the chest cavity. Eating as it went not only for itself but for the children.

Captain Morgan was going to make the perfect shelter until the storm was done and it was time to move on from the humans.

The End

Check out other great

Cryptid Novels!

J.H. Moncrieff

RETURN TO DYATLOV PASS

In 1959, nine Russian students set off on a skiing expedition in the Ural Mountains. Their mutilated bodies were discovered weeks later. Their bizarre and unexplained deaths are one of the most enduring true mysteries of our time. Nearly sixty years later, podcast host Nat McPherson ventures into the same mountains with her team, determined to finally solve the mystery of the Dyatlov Pass incident. Her plans are thwarted on the first night, when two trackers from her group are brutally slaughtered. The team's guide, a superstitious man from a neighboring village, blames the killings on yetis, but no one believes him. As members of Nat's team die one by one, she must figure out if there's a murderer in their midst—or something even worse—before history repeats itself and her group becomes another casualty of the infamous Dead Mountain.

Gerry Griffiths

CRYPTID ZOO

As a child, rare and unusual animals, especially cryptid creatures, always fascinated Carter Wilde. Now that he's an eccentric billionaire and runs the largest conglomerate of high-tech companies all over the world, he can finally achieve his wildest dream of building the most incredible theme park ever conceived on the planet... CRYPTID ZOO. Even though there have been apparent problems with the project, Wilde still decides to send some of his marketing employees and their families on a forced vacation to assess the theme park in preparation for Opening Day. Nick Wells and his family are some of those chosen and are about to embark on what will become the most terror-filled weekend of their lives—praying they survive. STEP RIGHT UP AND GET YOUR FREE PASS... TO CRYPTID ZOO

Check out other great

Cryptid Novels!

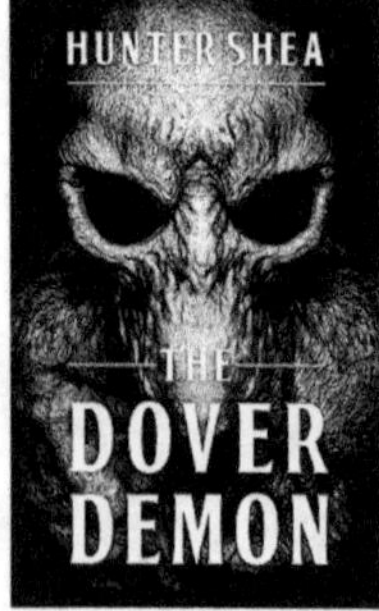

Hunter Shea

THE DOVER DEMON

The Dover Demon is real...and it has returned. In 1977, Sam Brogna and his friends came upon a terrifying, alien creature on a deserted country road. What they witnessed was so bizarre, so chilling, they swore their silence. But their lives were changed forever. Decades later, the town of Dover has been hit by a massive blizzard. Sam's son, Nicky, is drawn to search for the infamous cryptid, only to disappear into the bowels of a secret underground lair. The Dover Demon is far deadlier than anyone could have believed. And there are many of them. Can Sam and his reunited friends rescue Nicky and battle a race of creatures so powerful, so sinister, that history itself has been shaped by their secretive presence? "THE DOVER DEMON is Shea's most delightful and insidiously terrifying monster yet." – Shotgun Logic Reviews "An excellent horror novel and a strong standout in the UFO and cryptid subgenres." –Hellnotes "Non-stop action awaits those brave enough to dive into the small town of Dover, and if you're lucky, you won't see the Demon himself!" – The Scary Reviews PRAISE FOR SWAMP MONSTER MASSACRE "B-horror movie fans rejoice, Hunter Shea is here to bring you the ultimate tale of terror!" – Horror Novel Reviews "A nonstop thrill ride! I couldn't put this book down." – Cedar Hollow Horror Reviews

Armand Rosamilia

THE BEAST

The end of summer, 1986. With only a few days left until the new school year, twins Jeremy and Jack Schaffer are on very different paths. Jeremy is the geek, playing Dungeons & Dragons with friends Kathleen and Randy, while Jack is the jock, getting into trouble with his buddies. And then everything changes when neighbor Mister Higgins is killed by a wild animal in his yard. Was it a bear? There's something big lurking in the woods behind their New Jersey home.Will the police be able to solve the murder before more Middletown residents are ripped apart?

Check out other great

Cryptid Novels!

Ian Faulkner

CRYPTID

Be careful what you look for. You might just find it.1996. A group of 14 students walked into the trackless virgin forests of Graham Island, British Columbia for a three-day hike. They were never seen again. 2019. An American TV crew retrace those students' steps to attempt to solve a 23-year-old mystery.A disparate collection of characters arrives on the island. But all is not as it seems. Two of them carry dark secrets. Terrible knowledge that will mean death for some – but a fighting chance of survival for others. In the hidden depths of the forests – man is on the menu. Some mysteries should remain unsolved...

Eric S. Brown

LOCH NESS HORROR

The Order of the Eternal Light, a secret organization have foretold the end of the human race. In order to save all humanity, agents of the Order must locate the Loch Ness Monster and obtain a sample of its blood for within in it is the key to stopping the apocalypse but finding the monster will be no easy task.

www.ingramcontent.com/pod-product-compliance
Lightning Source LLC
LaVergne TN
LVHW020046110826
845155LV00029B/655

* 9 7 8 1 9 2 2 5 5 1 9 7 9 *